GO

The Murail siblings are a ... their own right – Marie-A... books worldwide, Elvire's very first novel was turned into a film and Lorris is well known for writing about his two passions: good food and science fiction. Together they make a truly formidable literary trio. When writing the Golem series, the siblings wanted not only to recapture the intensity and creativity of playing together as children, but also to write the kinds of books they would have liked when they were young. "It was like a game," says Elvire, the youngest. "It was a huge challenge, but we wanted to lose our individual voices and morph into a new, even better one. It worked so well that sometimes we had trouble remembering who had written what!" Her sister Marie-Aude adds, "It's so important to remember what you were like when you were young. It gets more difficult as you get older – you have to have your own children to get it back again!" It took two years to complete all five Golem books.

Now it is your turn to play…

GOLEM

This book is supported by the French Ministry for Foreign Affairs, as part of the Burgess programme headed for the French Embassy in London by the Institut Français du Royaume-Uni

Liberté • Égalité • Fraternité
RÉPUBLIQUE FRANÇAISE

5: Alias

Elvire, Lorris and Marie-Aude Murail
translated by Sarah Adams

WALKER BOOKS
AND SUBSIDIARIES
LONDON · BOSTON · SYDNEY · AUCKLAND

First published 2005 by Walker Books Ltd
87 Vauxhall Walk, London SE11 5HJ

2 4 6 8 10 9 7 5 3 1

Original Edition: *Golem 5 – Alias*
© 2002 Éditions Pocket Jeunesse,
a division of Univers Poche, Paris – France
Translation © 2005 Sarah Adams
Cover image © 2005 Guy McKinley

The right of Elvire, Lorris and Marie-Aude Murail to be
identified as authors of this work has been asserted by them
in accordance with the Copyright, Designs and Patents Act 1988

This book has been typeset in DeadHistory and M Joanna

Printed and bound in Great Britain
by Bookmarque Ltd, Croydon, Surrey

British Library Cataloguing in Publication Data:
a catalogue record for this book
is available from the British Library

ISBN 1-84428-618-5

www.walkerbooks.co.uk

Contents

LOADING...

In Golem: LEVEL 4:

Majid and his friends' dream trip to B Happy Land, the famous Swiss theme park, has turned into a nightmare. It all started so well, with an exciting helicopter ride and a visit to the House of Horror. But then things get out of hand: a witch tries to hypnotize them, they are chased down giant supermarket aisles by outsize furry animals, and Sebastian gets shot by girl-golem Natasha's deadly eraser-laser. And that's before they've even reached B Corp HQ, where Alias, the Master Golem, is about to blow up the entire building with everybody in it.

Only twenty minutes left and counting...

0%
10%
20%
30%
40%
50%
60
70%
80%
90

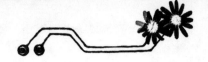

Safe and Sound?

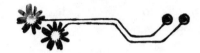

Nadia had four little humans on her hands and twenty minutes to leave the bunker. Twenty minutes to game over. Aisha, Majid, Samir and Sebastian wouldn't get a second chance. They were twelve and thirteen years old. They'd only ever known one set of graphics: the tower blocks of the Moreland Estate. If they weren't out of B Corp HQ in twenty minutes, they'd be stuck on level one for ever. Grey sky. Cold concrete.

And Nadia had run out of ideas.

The route she'd thought was etched in her memory had disappeared. She remembered the cries of horror, the gaping wounds, the terror-filled eyes. She could still see the splayed corpses, right there, in front of her.

"Miss?" Aisha asked. "Are they dead?"

Yes. They were dead. But Nadia no longer knew in what order they'd died. And right now, to get out of this maze, she needed to know. They had to get from bloodbath number 5 back to bloodbath number 4 and so on, until they reached what was left of the big glass door at the main entrance.

Corridors, halls, security doors, stairs … Nadia didn't recognize anything any more. She'd followed Natasha, panic-stricken and terrified. Now she had to take the same path, but in the opposite direction. On her own. Correction: with four children. And she'd never seen them like this before. Mute.

"Childwen, I think…"

Don't cry. Make a decision. Hadn't she already followed these red lines on the floor? Yes, but which way? Her eyes met Majid's. The kid was begging her to do something, to know the answer. He's counting on me, thought Nadia, he's counting on me so badly.

"Over there."

When she saw the glass doors with ghostly computers lined up behind them in the gloom, she knew she'd gone the wrong way. But she carried on. Nothing else for it.

Twenty minutes, Natasha had said. How much time was left? She didn't want to look at her watch. They'd just reached a huge open space, a chilled zone where hundreds of packages were stacked up. A dispatch warehouse. She definitely hadn't come this way.

"Childwen, I'm not sure…" She glanced desperately back down the long corridor. She had to make a decision. Fast.

"I've made a mistake. We've got to turn back. We're going to have to run fast, OK?"

But the children weren't listening. They didn't trust her any more.

"The truck!" Sebastian shouted. He climbed up into a forklift truck and frantically tried the controls.

"Leave it," said Samir. Shoving his friend out of the way, he got in the driver's seat and managed to start the engine. "Get in, everybody!"

They hurtled along for two hundred metres,

past walls of piled-up boxes. The underground warehouse seemed to go on and on. Nadia was standing on the platform at the back of the truck, clinging to Aisha as she peered into the darkness ahead. That's not the exit, she thought. Suddenly she saw a sign hanging from a chain. She recognized the stylized image of a forklift truck.

It was crossed out with a big red line.

"Thamir! Not that way! It's not allowed!"

"'Low it, man."

The truck and its five passengers tipped down onto a ramp. Slowly, ever so slowly, it picked up speed.

Samir clung to the steering wheel, and made it round the first two bends without mishap. Then the truck scraped against the wall. And suddenly smashed into it: once, twice. A third bump, more violent than the others, bounced it back towards the opposite wall, flinging out its passengers.

Nadia was the last to get up, rubbing her sore elbow. "Are you all wight, childwen?"

But they'd gone on without her, sliding down the ramp as if she was no longer part of the group. They fell over. They got up again. Nobody cried out. By the time she caught up, they'd reached an underground car park.

"It's the right one," Sebastian called out. He'd recognized his parents' camper van. No matter how big the car park, the Volkswagen was always easy to spot.

The keys were on the dashboard. As they headed out, all the barriers were raised, all doors open. Here, like everywhere else, Alias had unlocked everything.

The camper van exited the mountainside the way it had entered: by the north entrance. It emerged into moonlight on a section of road two hundred metres long.

The blast from the explosion was so powerful, Nadia momentarily lost control of the wheel. It was like the camper van wasn't on the road any more. Like it was flying. She couldn't see anything. Just a few reflections in the windscreen, a few snatched images in the rear-view mirror. A ball of fire. A giant shadow. The top part of the bunker lifting off like a saucepan lid, before crashing back down again.

Crushing everything.

She spared a thought for those still inside. Albert? Natasha? Hugh?

Nadia put her foot on the accelerator and shot down the deserted road. A few minutes later, she slammed on the brakes. There were two cars blocking the way. Police! About time. She couldn't keep this up much longer.

"We're saved!"

Three policemen made their way over, training their torches on the VW. Nadia saw the face of one of them pressed against the window. Then she couldn't see anything: he was blinding her with the light.

"I've got the childwen with me," she said through the lowered window. "Safe and sound."

The door opened. Nadia started to climb out. But a hand grabbed her arm and wrenched her from the driver's seat. She screamed. The policeman twisted her arm behind her back and flung her against the side of the VW. Her forehead hit the bodywork. She could feel hands all over her, on her sides, her stomach, her thighs. All three of them had surrounded her. One yanked her hair to make her turn her head. Torches were sweeping up and down her.

A man spoke. "It's her. It's Michelle."

She recognized that voice. Stefano! The playboy with the red convertible.

"The children! Get the children out!" somebody yelled.

Nadia was driven to Gruyères police station. She was taken into a room with bars on the window. Just like that. No explanation. Stunned, she collapsed on a chair. It felt like her day had started forty hours ago...

Somebody shook her roughly. "What is it? The weapon – what kind is it?"

The remains of a dream were still floating before her eyes. She was caught under the smoking rubble of a warehouse ravaged by fire. Nadia had never fallen asleep sitting on a chair before.

"They say it makes holes that won't close up again," said the man who was leaning over her. He shook her again and repeated his question. Urgently. "What is it?"

Nadia could feel the blood pounding in her head. In the muffled world where she was struggling, nothing seemed very urgent.

Then the man asked her something odd. "What organization do you belong to?"

She looked at him wearily. Only one thing mattered. "Where are the childwen?" she asked.

"They're safe."

Something wasn't right. Nadia could tell. From the way they were treating her, from the way this man was talking to her. But she was too exhausted to put up a fight.

"I'm not planning on conducting a full interrogation for the time being," said the man. "You know what interests me."

Nadia shook her head.

"Are we still in danger?" he asked. "More bombs?"

She shuddered. "Please," she whispered, "I want to go home."

The man was surprised. He sat down opposite her, his hands on his knees. "I'm Eberhardt," he said. "Michelle isn't your real name, is it?"

"No. It's Nadia Martin."

"There's something I simply don't understand. Why did you and your fellow terrorist hitch a lift?"

Nadia felt her body temperature drop several degrees. Her fellow terrorist?

"I mean, you already had a vehicle. That camper van's yours, isn't it?"

She nodded, then confessed, "Well, no, actually, it belongs to Sebathian's dad. Sebathian's one of the childwen."

This information confused Eberhardt even more. "Is he part of the network?"

"What network?"

Thinking Eberhardt was about to hit her, Nadia covered her face. Fortunately, his attention was diverted as the door opened and another man came in.

"Drop it," said the newcomer. "We've got the first autopsy report. This one's not for us." And then he added scornfully, "They're bringing in the BIB boys." He nodded in Nadia's direction. "She's to go into solitary. No more questions."

Nadia wondered if this was good news.

She lay down on the mattress in the cell and slept right through till the following day. At least, that was what she thought. But when she saw three meal trays that nobody had cleared away still on the floor, she realized she must have slept for longer.

Everything was cold. She swallowed a few mouthfuls of rice and emptied three beakers of water, one after the other.

An hour later, she met the BIB boys.

Tommy was Afro-Caribbean. Payne was blond. They were waiting for her in a comfortable room, without any bars on the window. They'd had their food trays too. There were leftover hamburgers and large Big B cola cans on the table. Tommy and Payne had travelled a long way, and it showed: crumpled faces, rumpled clothes.

"We work for the Big Investigation Bureau," announced Payne. "We were notified" – he looked at his watch – "fourteen hours ago. And here we are." He looked chuffed. He was perched on the edge of the table, his bottom framed by junk food. "As I'm sure you'll appreciate, we don't get called out for run-of-the-mill terrorism cases."

"We're here because of what we're about to show you," said Tommy, closing the blinds.

On the table, in the middle of all the discarded

packaging, was an old-fashioned slide projector. When Payne shone the first image onto the small wall screen, Nadia looked away. It showed the lifeless bodies of the B Corp cowboys slaughtered in the B Happy Land car park. The photos that followed were close-ups.

Tommy was standing next to the screen, with a pointer. "The projectile entered here, piercing the cheek, or malar bone, and severing the pterygoid muscles before exiting at the back of the skull, at the level of the petro-occipital suture, after causing exactly the sort of damage you would expect to the cerebral matter."

Nadia tried not to hiccup.

"There's a small incision at the entrance to these wounds – a very clean incision."

"Surgical," Payne added.

Click. Another image appeared on the screen. Another wound. Another trajectory.

"Not a drop of blood in those wounds," Tommy pointed out. "The projectile tunnels into the flesh like a drill. But a human head isn't a plank of wood. What we're seeing here, Miss Martin, is, by definition, impossible."

They both turned to face Nadia.

"The weapon isn't one we're familiar with," said Tommy.

"Although there are some similarities with the Annapolis affair in Maryland," Payne concluded.

"May 1990. A case that was never solved."

"Miss Martin," said Payne, "what is this weapon? Where does it come from?"

Nadia took a deep breath. And provided the only information she could. "An ewaser-laser."

Tommy nodded. "We were thinking along those lines."

"Were you acting under duress?" asked Payne.

Nadia widened her scared eyes and nodded. She'd have to play it very carefully. "That ... cweature is tewifying."

"What d'you know about her?" asked Tommy.

"She says her name's Natatha. But I don't think she's totally human."

The men glanced at each other. Clearly they'd already reached this conclusion.

"You're the only witness to what happened in the building," Tommy went on. "There were twenty-eight fatalities."

Nadia had one burning question, but she held back. She would have given anything to find out whether the fatalities included a tall muscly man with brown hair, and an overgrown teenager with an old-fashioned name... No, actually she'd rather not know.

"I've forgotten nearly everything," she whispered, trying her best to sound convincing. "I was totally under the contwol of that cweature. I just acted like a wobot. I can wemember scweaming, flashes of light, smoke ... and then ... and then ... I found the childwen. My students." She started sobbing, without having to try too hard.

Just then there was a knock at the door. It was Eberhardt. "We've got proof," he said, holding out a sheet of paper. "She's a terrorist based in Moreland Town."

"Yeah," said Payne absent-mindedly. He took the piece of paper and shooed Eberhardt away. He glanced at it, then turned back to Nadia. "The police have searched your home, Miss Martin. They found dangerous chemicals in your kitchen."

The ingredients Nadia had used to make tear-gas.

"I'm a science teacher. They're chemicals for my expewiments—"

"There's no need to justify yourself, Miss Martin," interrupted Tommy. "Where we come from, most teachers prefer to go to school armed."

"You've had a big shock," said Payne, putting a friendly hand on her shoulder. "You need to rest up. And we're going to do all we can to track down this creature before..." There was a lump in his throat. He carried on huskily. "Before she puts our whole civilization at risk."

"Payne gets very emotional," explained Tommy. "He can go a bit over the top." He looked at his watch. "We're going to have to break off this interview. We've asked to attend the autopsy of one of the victims. There's a lot at stake here."

"Are they going to keep me in pwison?" asked Nadia.

"It's not for us to decide," Payne replied. "But we're going to send you a Red Cross volunteer who'll be a great comfort to you."

"Miss Goody."

"Yes, Miss Goody," echoed Payne, as if her name alone was a great comfort.

Real People,
Virtual People

The moon was reflected in the waters of Lake Gruyère. How had Hugh got there? After the B Corp bunker had blown up, he'd headed off with Natasha: walking, stumbling, running, falling over. He didn't know if he was guilty or innocent. But he knew the woman who'd saved his life had killed people. That had been one of his last thoughts on the road leading down to the lake. He must have blacked out. She must have carried him.

He was alone now, propped against a tree. The mountain ridge opposite was black against the midnight blue sky. Far-off sirens echoed in the valley: the emergency services were arriving. Had Nadia got the children to safety? Had Albert got out of B Corp HQ alive? Hugh was trying to think of real people, made of flesh and blood like him. But he kept being tormented by...

"Natasha!"

Was she there in the dark? Or had she deserted him? Hugh made a supreme effort to cling onto the tree and stand up. Every now and then, another light went on in the valley. People who'd been woken by the explosion. He turned to face the forest and called out, "Natash... Aha!"

She was sitting in the grass, leaning against a rock, so rigid and still she looked like a robot waiting to be switched on. Her eyes were wide open, shining like stones in the moonlight.

She must be in down time, he thought. He didn't dare talk to her. It wasn't a living creature or a machine in front of him. It was something between a monster and nothing.

The eraser-laser was lying in the grass. Hugh stooped to pick it up. A hand locked around his wrist and he roared in terror.

Natasha had switched herself back on again.

"*Peowww! Peowww!*" she went feebly. She knew her

weapon was no longer operational. "Alias wants me to transfer my data."

Hugh was too tired to wonder what this meant. Natasha stood up. He watched her snatch up her weapon and head towards the lake. In a flash, he realized what she was up to. She was going to make contact with the water, in order to disconnect and go back inside the computer. But the computer was now in Orwell's hands!

"That's water, Natasha! You'll lose a life. You've only got two left."

"I have to transfer my data. Alias is waiting."

Every so often she had to download all the information she'd stored about the real world into the electric blue computer, as if she was just a floppy disk.

"Stay with me," Hugh begged her.

"Calimero is my ally," she said, sounding almost thoughtful.

How could he make her understand that Orwell would pretend to be Calimero? He stood in front of her, blocking her path. "I haven't got the computer any more. Orwell has. He's the master of B Corp, and he will pretend to be your ally."

"Hugh."

"Yes?"

"Hugh."

"What?"

"Hugh."

Nothing else. She was busy assimilating the new data.

"It's good to think things over, but it's not helpful when I'm trying to discuss them with you," he grumbled.

Half a minute later, Natasha stepped to the side. She wanted to set off towards the lake again.

"I am going to transfer my data."

"You've totally missed the point!" he shouted. "Orwell will pretend to be me: are you stupid or what?" It was all he could do not to shake her.

"Hugh has not got the computer any more," Natasha said. "I have to warn Alias." She looked at Hugh as if waiting for confirmation.

"Alias can handle it alone. Stay with me." As soon as Natasha showed the slightest sign of human behaviour, he fell in love with her again.

"I cannot stay."

"Of course you can. You're free, aren't you?"

Natasha pushed back her blonde fringe and the word EMET was revealed branded on her tanned skin. "Alias will give me my freedom if you finish the game."

"D'you know what Alias is?" Hugh was starting to lose his temper. "Artificial Logical Intelligence for Absolute Security. It's the security system developed by B Corp."

"Fatal error. Alias is the Master Golem."

Were they talking about the same Alias?

Unexpectedly, Natasha put her hands on his shoulders and pressed her lips against his. Coming into contact with her now only produced a slight tingling. And the benefits easily outweighed the mild inconvenience. Hugh's legs gave way and Natasha had to support him.

"I have to get some sleep," he muttered. Then he glanced at her and translated: "I've got to press *pause*. But don't go anywhere near the water, OK?"

"Is there another option?"

"Stay here. I need you."

"Click on HELP."

Hugh looked up at the sky, but no menu bar dropped down out of the darkness.

"We're in the real world, Natasha, and I *really* need you."

She placed two fingers on his lips. He smiled.

"Do you want me to kiss you?" she asked.

He hesitated, stretched out his arms and closed them around her. "See, this is how real people connect."

When an electric current surged through him, he nearly let go. But this time it was Natasha who held him tight. He felt they were pooling their resources, like two machines that had been networked. Real and virtual, gamer and warrior, love and power. Slowly they pulled apart.

"I'm not tired any more," he said. "You've rebooted me."

Far away, in a modest suburban flat, somebody was thinking about him. Mrs Mullins was worried. Her son had been gone over twenty-four hours now, and she'd had no news. From the moment her alarm clock had gone off at seven, until her bedtime, which she kept postponing, she'd been waiting for a phone call. Her only comfort was a kind of blue-eyed lizard that purred whenever she looked at it.

Bubble was as good as tamed now, and Mrs Mullins had got into the habit of talking to him.

"The thing is, you see, Hugh wasn't behaving normally when he left."

Bubble purred. *Merr merr…*

He had plenty of admiration for the boss with the broom. Even though he thought longingly of the days when he'd have terrorized her by drawing himself up to his full height of two metres.

Mrs Mullins scratched the carpet. "Ickle-lickle…"

Bubble was timid but he liked this game. He edged closer and put a paw on the boss's hand. Then pulled it back. And put it on her hand again. Each time, Mrs Mullins got a tiny shock. She'd realized she didn't need to worry about an allergic reaction. This was electricity, no two ways about it. The creature was fizzing with electric current. Which meant it wasn't an animal, not even an exotic one, as Hugh had claimed. So was it a toy, or a robot? Bubble seemed to be nearly as independent as a living creature. Except that no living creature could cope with two hundred and thirty volts being pumped into it for a whole hour. It did Bubble a heap of good, though.

"Ickle-lickle…"

The little dragon got so excited by the game, he lost his head. His blue eyes turned red and, with all his might, he breathed out an evil flame. Pained and surprised, Mrs Mullins gave a shriek. There was a brown mark on her hand, like a burn. Bubble trotted off under the armchair to hide, next to the skirting board.

Mrs Mullins was upset by this display of aggression. You can't trust anybody, she told herself, which her job as a psychologist should have taught her long ago. She decided to go to bed with a book. As she was setting her clock radio for the following morning, she accidentally pressed the wrong button and switched on the radio.

"Good evening. This is the ten o'clock news. We're going straight to Lausanne, where we are joined by our Swiss correspondent, Quentin Dapper. What's the latest on this afternoon's attack, Quentin?"

Mrs Mullins was about to turn the radio off, but she paused for a moment.

"Thank you, Mark. Five fatalities have now been reported. It appears the victims were B Happy Land employees, involved in a lasso demonstration in the car park of the world-famous theme park."

B Happy Land! She froze. That was where Hugh had gone.

"The police are urgently seeking two young women, whose descriptions have been broadcast locally. Earlier this afternoon, one of them opened fire. According to eyewitnesses she is, and I quote: 'a sort of Lara Croft, but blonde'. We're expecting more details shortly. For now, the talk is of an uprising by sacked employees…"

Mrs Mullins held her breath. Why should there be a link between this macabre news item and Hugh's silence?

The newsreader said, "Thank you, Quentin. Back home, workers in Toolinex…"

She switched the radio off. She'd made up her mind. For too long she hadn't wanted to admit something was going on. Now, whatever Hugh was up to, it was time to find out.

He'd lied to her. About an animal that wasn't one. About that girl he'd introduced as Natasha Duran. Who *was* she? Mrs Mullins shuddered as she remembered the strange creature. Wasn't *she* a sort of Lara Croft? And what about that Joke Lulu had told her was hiding out in the quarry – who was he?

It was dark and windy. The rain was lashing against the windows. But nothing would stop Mrs Mullins. She grabbed her car keys, put on her boots and cagoule and set out.

It was chucking it down. Fighting against the gusts of rain, she made her way towards the entrance to the quarry. What was she looking for, if not the truth?

"Joke! Joke!" she called out.

She was answered by a sort of wailing that sounded like a cross between a baby crying and a mooing calf that had lost its mother. She switched on her torch and headed into the quarry. The water reached her ankles.

Joke had retreated inside his tunnel. Slumped against the wall, he'd turned back into a wrinkled, transparent hologram. The ray of light caught him by chance. He shuddered and started wailing again.

Mrs Mullins nearly dropped her torch. "Goodness me! What is *that*?" she whispered.

The white, faintly human-shaped creature made a plaintive noise. "Friend, friieeennnnddd…"

Mrs Mullins stood still for a few seconds, lighting the creature with her torch. Its outline was hazy, as if its edges dissolved into thin air. But it had a face of sorts, with stitched eyes and a hideous gash instead of a mouth. And it seemed in such a bad way that, gradually, she calmed down.

"Joke?" she called.

"Friend," he answered.

He kept repeating this word, which made her feel peculiarly sad. And powerless. What could she do for the poor creature? Wait a minute. Majid and Lulu knew about Joke, and so did Hugh…

"Of course!"

That was it. She'd already seen something like it on her son's computer. Hugh had mentioned a bug or a virus that popped up on the screen at the most annoying times. And he'd referred to this unwanted bug as Joke. Natasha with her weapon that definitely wasn't a toy slung over her shoulder, Bubble recharging himself in electricity sockets, and now Joke… Where did they come from? Another world? Somewhere beyond? And what did they want?

Mrs Mullins's curiosity got the better of her and she drew closer. Her torch brushed against Joke. It vanished instantly, and an electrical discharge sent her flying backwards. As she tried to stand up again in the dark, she saw Joke crackling and swelling up, emitting a blue light.

"Me got munchies," he said.

Mrs Mullins was terrified. Clutching the wall for support, she stumbled out of the tunnel. In the main dugout, she slipped over several times in pools of water. Finally she flopped into her car. The real meaning of a word she was used to writing down had just dawned on her: *traumatized*. She started the engine, and the radio kicked in too.

"This is Quentin Dapper reporting from Gruyères. Well, it's certainly an apocalyptic scene I'm watching here. B Corp HQ, described as a destruction-proof bunker, has literally folded in on itself. In fact, I'm going to have to leave the area shortly, because further explosions are expected."

"There've been suggestions of an attack by anti-globalists: has this been confirmed?"

"Well, for the time being, the only link is to this afternoon's events at B Happy Land. The talk is still of two young women with contacts inside the building."

With a faraway look in her eyes, Mrs Mullins switched off the radio and headed slowly home.

Back in her bedroom, the sight of Bubble lying under her armchair made her burst into tears. It was too much. Taking a few deep breaths, she managed to pull herself together. But when the phone rang, she shrieked. Bubble, who was just crawling out from his hiding place, flattened himself against the skirting board.

"Mum?" said an airy voice on the other end. "Am I calling too late?"

Mrs Mullins was trembling. "It's nice to hear from you, dear," she stammered. "Are you all right?"

"Great. I'm calling from a phone box. I'm still in Switzerland. I think I'll … I think I'll drive back through the night. But don't wait up for me."

"Drive sensibly," whispered Mrs Mullins.

"Sure. Oh … and by the way, d'you mind if I bring a girlfriend with me?" Hugh was trying to sound light and breezy.

"A girlfriend?" she echoed, fearing the worst.

"Yes... You've already met her, in fact. Natasha Duran!"

Does a Babe Make a Good Daughter-in-Law?

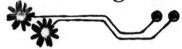

Hugh wasn't an experienced driver, so, at night, at the wheel of a stolen car, he wasn't exactly relaxed. Luckily he'd passed a deserted customs checkpoint before the police barriers had been set up. He was heading for Moreland Town now, with Natasha in the boot. At least he knew she wouldn't get car sick. She was in one of her down-time moments.

As he got closer to his flat, he started thinking about what he was going to say to his mum. He'd tell her Natasha was his girlfriend. That they planned to rent a flat together. While he was struggling to find the right words, he realized he'd never even thought about leaving his mother before.

He parked in a quiet side street and opened the boot. Natasha got out, hair and make-up as immaculate as a Hollywood actress playing a journalist in a war zone.

When he reached his apartment block, Hugh saw the lights in the flat were still on.

Mrs Mullins had fallen asleep with her clothes on. Tucked snugly into a fold of the duvet, Bubble was digesting his kilowatts.

The sound of the key in the lock made Mrs Mullins sit up with a start. Bubble leapt into the air and let out a series of excited squeaks. He could detect the presence of another virtual being.

"Mother?" Hugh called out uncertainly.

Mrs Mullins came out of her bedroom with her hand on her forehead, because she had a migraine.

"I'm sorry it's so early…" Hugh tried to give his mother a peck on the cheek, but she was staring at Natasha and pushed him away.

"Mother is an ally?" asked Natasha.

Bubble had arrived hot on the boss's heels and was jumping about and squeaking. Hugh sensed things were getting out of hand. He turned to

Natasha to try and reassure her. "Mother is very kind." Then he turned back to his mum. "You don't mind if Natasha calls you Mother? She likes to feel part of the family."

"Mother is an ally?" Natasha asked again.

While they were talking, Bubble was making as much noise as he could in the hope that Natasha would pick him up.

"Don't waste your breath, Hugh," replied Mrs Mullins. "I know the truth."

"What truth?"

"About Joke and Bubble and Natasha. They run on electricity."

"Well, kind of," he admitted. "Anyway, it's best I find a flat for Natasha and me. We'd just end up getting on your nerves."

Mrs Mullins gave her son and the creature next to him a horrified look. "Have you *any* idea what you're saying?"

Natasha aimed her eraser-laser and made *peowwww! peowwww!* sound effects, like a kid playing war games.

Bubble joined in. *Squeak squeak!*

"Look, just shut it, will you?" said Hugh, losing his temper and giving the little dragon a gentle kick.

Natasha picked Bubble up and crushed him defiantly between her breasts. Mrs Mullins took a few deep breaths and calmed down slightly. "Just tell me one thing, Hugh." She lowered her voice so he could hardly hear. *"Has she killed people?"*

"It's not her fault! She's virtual. She has to obey Alias."

"And who would that be?"

Hugh pulled a face. He'd like to know too. "It's something in my computer." Intrigued, he glanced at the little dragon, who was making faint purring noises. Natasha was standing totally still, registering the final data relating to Mother-Ally.

"The car!" he exclaimed suddenly. He had to hide it. The stolen vehicle with its Swiss number plate was bound to attract attention.

"Why don't you park it at the quarry?" suggested Mrs Mullins. "Joke's already there, but..." Her son didn't seem to have a problem with any of these strange creatures.

He nodded and headed towards the door.

"Aren't you taking her with you?" His mother pointed to Natasha.

"She'll be calm now. If she reconnects, just tell

her Mother is an ally. And if she asks for me, tell her Hugh's gone to the next level but he'll be back to finish the game."

This put Mrs Mullins in a spin. It was like trying to get to grips with the instructions for a computer game. She repeated feverishly, "Mother is going to reconnect at the next level and Hugh ... Hugh... What was it?"

The young teacher shook his head. "Make an effort, Mum."

When her son had gone, Mrs Mullins tiptoed around so as not to rouse Natasha.

"Mother is my ally," said the girl-golem sharply.

Mrs Mullins shrieked and clutched her chest. She started to gabble frantically. "Yes, that's right, we're allies. I'm Hugh's mother – just think how well we're going to get on! Did you have a good trip? I went to Switzerland with my husband, but we're talking at least fifteen years ago. It must have changed a lot. Why don't you sit down? I was going to make some coffee. Would you like some? No, of course not, how stupid of me! There's an electric socket just behind you."

Natasha didn't answer. Was she busy registering all the data provided by Mother-Ally?

"Hugh?"

"He's gone to ... get some bread. Er, no, to the next level. To park the car. Are you sure you don't want some electricity?"

They were definitely having communication problems.

"Where is Hugh?" Natasha asked again, pointing her eraser-laser at Mrs Mullins.

"Just be careful with that. You'll end up hurting somebody. There *are* other ways of expressing your aggression, you know. You should try articulating your emotions."

"*Peowww! Peowww!*"

"That's a start."

Now she thought about it, Natasha wasn't so different from some of the disturbed children she had come across. She dug out a few blank sheets of paper and some felt-tip pens. "Here you are. Why don't you draw a pretty picture for when Hugh gets back?"

Natasha sat down at the table, with Bubble on her lap. Slowly she put the eraser-laser down and picked up a pen. "*Peowww! Peowww!*" she went, pointing it at Hugh's mother.

"No, not like that." Carefully Mrs Mullins took the pen from Natasha and drew a little stick man. "There you go. Now draw Alias for me."

"Alias is my master," said Natasha, grabbing the pen.

"It's never a good idea to blame other people," said Mrs Mullins. Then she fell silent. Natasha was busy covering the page with letters and numbers, without even looking at what she was doing.

ag/4215 : wj
lt.doc. 576
ihghto/bn.doc
a/6758439
st.dic/em12
@jdr/25895632 fs

She's a bit limited, thought Mrs Mullins. But at least she knows how to keep herself busy. She went and made herself a cup of coffee. When she came back, the whole page was covered in letters and numbers. With a glazed look in her eyes, Natasha kept saying over and over again, "Hugh, Hugh."

"He's coming, he's coming," soothed Mrs Mullins. "He's going to be *so* happy when he sees the lovely … er … drawing you've done for him!"

"Where is Hugh?"

"Goodness me, she's exhausting."

Hugh was at the deserted quarry. Having parked the car, he went into the tunnel in search of Joke. He hadn't seen him since their encounter in the basements. Not a happy memory.

Joke was stuck to the wall, like some kind of gooey, transparent substance. Mrs Mullins had fed him, but his appetite for electricity was insatiable.

Hugh hurried back outside. He remembered Samir's conviction that Joke and Lulu were connected. If one of them grew weak, the other also lost their strength. Little Lulu must be very feeble these days, thought Hugh. Where was she? Oh yes, in hospital. He should go back inside and feed Joke the battery from the stolen car…

But being in love, he charged home instead. He pounded the ground as he ran all the way back to the flat. *Na-ta-sha Na-ta-sha…*

"Natasha!" he yelled, flinging open the front door.

"Everything's fine. She's been very good," Mrs Mullins assured him.

The girl-golem went up to Hugh and held out a sheet of paper. "Natasha has done a lovely drawing for Hugh," she said.

Hugh glanced at it in astonishment.

gbh.doc//25487269
oww/4785:gkoir

"Tell her it's lovely," whispered Mrs Mullins.

"What? Yes, absolutely… It's lovely, Natasha."

lst.doc/12588795
emm806/ stz
mrstt : 12587958

He frowned. Somewhere in this jumble was a clue, but he didn't know where.

"She didn't want anything to eat."

"Eat?" Hugh panicked. "But you mustn't give her anything to eat!"

Mrs Mullins mouthed silently, "Electricity."

Hugh started laughing. "No, no, she doesn't need it. Joke and Bubble are bugs. They have to keep recharging themselves. But she…" He smiled. "She's fully operational." It was clear he meant drop-dead gorgeous.

He took another look at the "lovely drawing" and suddenly twigged.

"Mum, it's coded. It's a message!"

But he didn't get a chance to explain. The doorbell rang.

"Are you expecting anybody?" Mrs Mullins asked.

He shook his head. It rang again. And again, several times, in quick succession. Who was there: enemy or ally?

Hugh opened the door. Just a crack…

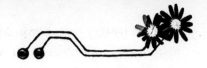

Doing It the B Corp Way

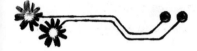

Back on track! was the new B Corp slogan after the bunker had been blown up.

Get rich fast was Bernard Martin-Webber's slogan. The manager of Moreland Town Big B Stores had been invited by B Corp to a training day run by Mr Pitch, from the communications agency Pitch & Spoke. Which was why, on this particular morning, he found himself in the multinational's glamorous city premises, looking aggressively around at the assembled crowd, wondering whose toes he had to tread on to climb higher up the B Corp ladder.

He recognized Alicia, the woman with severe

grey hair who had terrorized him when she'd inspected his store.

"Good morning, Miss Pennypinch," he boomed, spotting her blue name badge and realizing why she was so attached to her first name.

"Oh, hello," she said icily. "I'm afraid you'll have to excuse me. I think it's starting."

Sure enough, everybody was taking their seats. Two female workshop facilitators were handing out notepads and biros stamped with the B Corp logo. BMW read through the morning's agenda. They were going to start by listening to Mr Pitch's presentation on "B Corp Phylosophy". He tried not to snigger at the spelling.

Mr Pitch made his entrance. He was very tall and rather stooped, from having to bend over when he talked to people. His dark handsome eyes were sad: he'd have won lots of prizes at dog shows in the "depressed cocker" category. Which reminded BMW: now his divorce had come through, he needed to buy a dog. He was torn between a Labrador and a pit bull. By the time he'd settled on a husky (very trendy), they were already at the end of the presentation. Mr Pitch was talking about B Corp's target buyers, the company's ideal consumers: teenagers.

"The B Teen," gabbled Mr Pitch, "consumes an enormous part of the family budget. If you've got the teenager, you've got the whole family." He suddenly clapped his hands. "I'm going to ask you to close your eyes and visualize your B Teen..."

BMW looked around him. His neighbours had closed their eyes obediently to get a clearer picture of a Big B teenager in his or her B Sporty trainers, climbing onto a B Sporty moped. BMW shut his eyes and saw – horror of horrors – Samir staring rudely at him. Irritated, the manager of Moreland Town Big B Stores shook his head to dislodge the image. With some difficulty, he managed to picture a nice-looking blond kid straight out of the Price Shrinkers catalogue.

"When you've visualized your B Teen," Mr Pitch went on, "focus all your energy into thinking: B Corp is cool, B Corp is yoof." When Mr Pitch said *yoof* he brought his front teeth down over his lower lip. He looked like he was about to blow a raspberry. "Yoof and cool," he said again. "We are yoof and cool."

BMW, who was starting to lose his hair, as well as getting serious love handles, repeated earnestly, "I am yoof and cool."

After lunch, the participants were asked to check the colour of the badge pinned to their jacket. BMW had a blue one.

"Blue badges over here, please!" a workshop employee called out.

BMW felt his heart race, just like one of his customers scratching a golden voucher at the checkout and seeing the letters WIN... Had he got the winning badge? He noticed straight off there were just ten of them following the facilitator through a series of showrooms. Alicia Pennypinch was the only woman.

But the surprises weren't over yet. Like everybody else, BMW was made to go through a metal detector gate, where he set off the alarm. He had to empty his pockets and hand his keys and nail scissors over to a security guard sitting in front of a control screen. Then he entered the B Corp directors' boardroom. Below a giant chandelier there was an equally giant green table, with the

B Corp logo emblazoned in the middle.

"Take a seat, sir," said the workshop facilitator.

There was a small name card in front of each place. BMW read: *Herman Scoff – Big B Foods, Alicia Pennypinch – Big B Supermarkets, Alan Slick – B Oil,* as well as *Professor Exploitem – Big B Research.* He went round the table until he found a card that said simply: *Bernard Martin-Webber.* He was about to sit down, when he got the shock of his life. The card next to his read: *Mr William.* The boss of B Corp was going to sit next to him! To curb his rising panic, BMW counted the chairs. Thirteen. Two were empty: Mr William's and the one next to it.

Once everybody was seated, there was silence as people pretended to leaf through their notepads or flick away specks of dust from the spotless bottle-green desk blotters.

The door opened again and a man with greying hair entered. He was so bland-looking, there were no words to describe him. But everybody got to their feet to greet him.

"Mr William sends his apologies," Orwell greeted his audience. "He's running rather late." He sat down in the empty seat next to Mr William's.

"But we can start without him."

Everybody nodded.

"I'd like to hear from each of you about how your divisions are doing." Orwell stared at Herman Scoff.

Without any further prompting, the president of Big B Foods piped up. "As you know, Mr Orwell, there's a Big Burger outlet opening somewhere in the world every five minutes."

Mr Pitch, who was still present, raised his hand to add his yoof take. "Teens *love* eating food that's greasy and sugary, which is exactly what's on offer at Big Burger."

"Thanks to us, one American teenager in four is obese," said Orwell coolly. "And we're confident of achieving a similar result here within five or six years."

This kind of sick humour was Mr William's trademark, but none of the B Corp directors knew how to react to Orwell, who added, "When these teenagers become adults, we'll have a serious public health problem on our hands."

After some hesitation, BMW decided to look concerned. Orwell gave a cruel chuckle. "But we've found the answer. How far have you got with your slimming pill research, Professor Exploitem?"

"We're conducting our first human trials," the professor replied.

Actually, he was talking about trials on children. Fifty orphans from Bondebarwa who'd been fattened up for the cause.

"We'd like to be sure the product is totally harmless before we put it on the market."

"Is it still on schedule for next year?" Orwell pressed him.

"Er … yes… That should give us enough time to reduce the side effects."

The side effects included the deaths of ten orphans. But they *were* the youngest. So far the older ones were OK.

"And what about you, Mr Slick?" continued Orwell. "Have you managed to get the conservationists to calm down?"

B Corp had built a petrochemical factory in between a retirement home and a nursery school. Ecologists maintained the factory might explode.

"We're going to have to make a few concessions."

"Absolutely," Orwell agreed. "Get the DANGER

ZONE signs repainted." Then he turned to a man with a brick-coloured complexion and bulging veins who looked fit to burst at any moment. "No more problems with our suppliers, Sir Andrew?"

"We've had to cut our overheads a bit," Sir Andrew Slash admitted. "So a day's labour costs us less than a pound, and a pair of B Sporty trainers costs a hundred and twenty." He guffawed. "We're doing very nicely, thank you."

There wasn't much likelihood of the ten-year-old children who made the B Sporty trainers in the distant factories of Tadbukistan demanding a pay rise.

"And what about the factory that caught fire?" enquired Alicia.

A fire had broken out in one of the dodgy warehouses where the children worked, resulting in twelve fatalities and forty injured.

"We've offered our condolences to the families involved," Sir Andrew responded.

"Ah, yes," Orwell whispered, "I wonder if you could tell us, Miss Pennypinch, what's in the pipeline to replace our farting goo range?"

"We're going to launch the Disgustings," said Alicia with fake enthusiasm. She took out two small plastic characters from her bag: one was green and throwing up over himself, the other was brown and crouched in a position that left little to the imagination.

"They're going to be everywhere from next year," she announced confidently. "You'll find them as computer games, cartoons, plastic figures and swap cards. Kids'll love them."

"Parents'll hate them," BMW retorted.

"Excellent!" exclaimed Pitch. "There's our slogan: *Your parents'll hate them.*"

But Orwell didn't look overly impressed by the two plastic prototypes. "I'll discuss the project with Mr William, Miss Pennypinch." He clearly had no intention of doing anything of the sort.

BMW chuckled to himself. Pennypinch was stuffed, and the Disgustings with her. Then he felt Orwell staring at him and quickly tried to look as yoof as possible.

Moron, thought Orwell. "Gentlemen," he went on, ignoring Alicia, "B Corp has just been through a terrible ordeal with the explosion of the Gruyères HQ. We're a prime target for terrorists, and nobody's pretending otherwise. But we're also aware, gentlemen, that B Corp has never been more powerful…" Orwell's eyes flashed at the thought of the electric blue computer that was now his.

He exited to feeble applause.

Alone in his office, Orwell stroked the keyboard of the electric blue computer. The screen came to life again and the following instruction was displayed:

Enter your name.

Orwell typed **Calimero**, knowing full well what would happen next. The gamer's name launched Golem. But it was the game as Albert had invented it, nothing more.

What did he have to do to make those virtual characters burst out from the screen? He was fearful of being betrayed if he handed the computer to his team of specialists. He hadn't told anybody about it, not even the representatives from the Big Investigation Bureau, and he wanted to silence everybody who *did* know.

Which left Albert. They hadn't found his body in the debris of the bunker. If anybody could get something out of this computer and this game, he could. But how was Orwell going to get hold of the young computer programmer? His lips stretched into a nasty smile. Nadia Martin was in his power, and Nadia Martin was linked to Albert. But what sort of link was it?

The red indicator light on the intercom started flashing and the distant voice of his secretary could be heard.

"Mr Orwell?"

"Yes?" said Orwell menacingly. He wasn't supposed to be disturbed unless it was very important.

"There's somebody who wants to talk to you about … about Calimero."

"Who is it?" Orwell was suddenly alert.

"Albert!" a male voice announced into the intercom.

Orwell smiled sadistically. So Albert had just turned himself in to B Corp! In a flash he realized why.

Albert was in love with Nadia Martin.

It would be a trade-off: Golem's secret in return for the girl.

alias@golem.seq12.npc

Two men were glaring at each other across the office. Two men who hated each other so much, they were this close to coming to blows.

"So you're not dead then," said Orwell.

Albert shrugged. He wasn't just alive and well, he'd even changed his clothes. Not bad going for a man on the run. "D'you know where Nadia Martin is?"

According to the media, the search was still on.

Orwell looked deep into Albert's eyes. Oh yes. This idiot was in love, all right. He gave a leisurely smile. "I might know something," he admitted.

Albert's hands gripped the arm of the chair so

tight his knuckles turned white. "I know something too."

"So let's trade," sneered Orwell.

"Prove you've got Nadia."

"You're in luck. Miss Goody sent me an update only this morning."

Orwell took a photo out of a file and pushed it towards Albert. It showed Nadia sitting in a chair, hunched and dazed. Towering behind her was a woman who was nearly six feet tall, holding a newspaper. The main headline was the collapse of B Corp HQ.

"What have you done to her?"

Orwell's evil smile got even wider. "Your girl-friend was a bit shaken up by what happened, and B Corp is offering her the best therapy: plenty of rest. Miss Goody is there to take care of her."

The woman behind Nadia was wearing a strange outfit, consisting of a long dress made out of thick material, and a veil. An old-fashioned nurse? Or a nun? Whatever her vocation, she knew how to smile flashing all her teeth.

Albert handed the photo back to Orwell, mut-tering, "Not my type." But the photo had had an impact. He was worried about Nadia's mental well-being. "I know what's happened inside my computer," he said.

Orwell lounged back in his chair and pretended to look distracted. Albert gave him a quick recap of what Alias was: a security system designed to defend B Corp against any kind of intrusion. Its job was to oversee everything going on in the B Corp bunker, and it was inside every B Corp computer, ready to fight any viruses and hackers. So it kept an eye on Golem too, the game Albert had been fine-tuning on his electric blue computer.

"B Corp asked me to insert subliminal messaging into the game. But Alias was never told about the decision, which was taken at the highest level."

When Albert secretly inserted the subliminal message Buy Big Brand farting goo, Alias thought it was being attacked. From the inside. The enemy was B Corp itself. And that was why, with Natasha's help, it had destroyed HQ.

"Well, you've got that off pat," Orwell cut him short. "But it doesn't explain anything. How come the Golem characters can get out of your computer? And it is your computer. It's your game."

"D'you know the golem legend?"

Orwell gave a slight wave of his hand and Albert continued.

"In the sixteenth century, in the Prague ghetto, Rabbi Loeb decided to make a servant by modelling it out of clay. He wrote the word EMET, meaning 'truth' in Hebrew, on its forehead, and gave life to it. But the golem kept getting bigger and bigger, and it destroyed the ghetto. The same thing that happened to Rabbi Loeb has happened to me. Golem got away…"

Orwell snorted. "That's ridiculous."

Albert was shaking with anger. But he had to convince Orwell. He didn't have any choice.

"It may sound absurd to you, Orwell, but Alias has reached such a high level of intelligence that it's been able to use my game to destroy B Corp. There was a strong similarity between its role as a slave to the system and the golem's own servitude. But there's a difference between you and the gamer, Orwell. A difference I programmed. You see, the gamer isn't Golem's real master. The gamer is in fact its ally, playing to win the golem's freedom. That's why Alias contacted Hugh Mullins, the gamer who had my computer. Alias made Mullins its ally, the person who can win its freedom. Calimero is both Hugh's gamer name and the password to make the golem come out."

Orwell gave the electric blue computer a smouldering look. He'd typed that word a hundred times. "It doesn't work."

"It doesn't work because Natasha – Hugh's golem – has escaped from the computer. But it'll work if we make another golem."

Orwell couldn't disguise his growing interest. He leant over his desk towards Albert. "What other golem?"

"Your call."

Orwell slid back in his chair, more puffed up and power crazy than ever. A golem. A golem of his choice. A golem that would call him master!

After escaping from the bunker, Albert had made his way back to Moreland Town. He'd rung the Mullinses' doorbell and had been relieved to find Hugh still alive. The young teacher had showed him what Natasha had written and he'd only just managed to decode. At first glance it looked like a meaningless series of letters and numbers, some kind of computer language. But all you had to do was take the first letter of each line to get the acrostic and read the following message: *alias@golem.seq12.npc*.

Albert realized straight away that Alias was setting up a meeting for the gamer in Golem. The rest was just as obvious, but he didn't want to say anything to Hugh. That way, if the young teacher fell into B Corp's hands again, he wouldn't be able to give anything away.

Now, with his fingers resting on the keyboard, Albert closed his eyes briefly. He was under constant camera surveillance, so he was going to have to be careful. Slowly he typed in the password that launched the game. **Calimero**. The little warrior appeared on the screen, helmet gleaming. He spun around a chain with a spiky golden ball at the end, and a deep voice rumbled, "*Golemmmm*." It was the opening sequence of the game Albert had invented.

He knew the following stages off by heart and reached sequence 12 without any problem: seq12.npc. He was in Golemia, the heroic fantasy capital where knights, witches, elves and dragons rubbed shoulders. He just had to find what the experts call, in computer jargon, an NPC or non-playing character. Sequence 12 took place in Taliva Square, on market day. There were lots of characters: vendors, thieves and travellers.

It was in this sequence that the gamer had to find an NPC who would give the little warrior a cryptic clue to send him on the right path. Albert clicked on a witch and got her to talk. Then, because he knew the answer to the clue, he made for the Golden Goose Inn, where he was attacked. After a series of traps and fights, the little warrior reached sequence 37, where the pile of pixels was waiting for him inside the palace. Albert realized he was on the wrong track and went back to sequence 12. His meeting was there and nowhere else.

For a moment, tiredness made him close his eyes. He'd thought he had the answer. But was he mistaken? He blinked and surveyed the screen absent-mindedly.

Suddenly he knew what to do. Something had changed in the graphics he was so familiar with. He set to work examining square centimetre by square centimetre.

"Bingo."

Between a tree and a wall, there was a tiny character he hadn't programmed, a sort of gnome with a beard and a hat, holding a watering can. The arrow on the cursor had become a hand. Albert just had to click on the dwarf. Would it spring to life and start talking? Would it give away Alias's secret? Albert glanced surreptitiously at the camera filming him. Then, trying to look like a moody gamer about to mess up for the umpteenth time, he clicked. The graphics disappeared and a series of numbers and letters appeared on the screen.

```
ild.doc/ ftc12478
ahx/@de468597
mfcod-125xxxnbfai2835
ajfjeidj.doc/djeifjhgz9uhfa9
lfjpaigpa94joajft0958/jkfao8to21
indioaur298/jfa9759827ncfqaoz75982
avnqsotu9823hgf034/ja098t6k
sv?ae4o9t8bncvqoiuhgtnvloajuit84
```

Albert went hot and cold.

Alias was putting in an appearance on the screen: I *am Alias*. That unimaginable being was there, ready to talk. All Albert had to do was answer in the same vertical way, couching the message in fake computer jargon.

Still using the acrostic layout, it was his turn to introduce himself: I am Calimero.

How long could the programmer and his computer communicate in this way before Orwell got suspicious?

That night, stretched out on his bunk, Albert went over what he'd learnt. Alias thought he was an ally, no doubt about that. In answer to the question *What does Alias want?* the answer had been: To destroy B Corp. Alias had understood that destroying the bunker at Gruyères and killing Mr William wasn't enough. B Corp still existed, in the virtual world and the real one. Alias wanted its freedom and it had the means to destroy B Corp. It could introduce itself into all of the multinational's computer systems and drop bombs, otherwise known as viruses. It could hack into the organization's business sites, re-route money from its bank accounts, devalue its share price on the stock market, trigger an economic crisis, make thousands of people unemployed, even topple governments.

B Corp had given life to an enemy as powerful as itself. Alias had the seeds of Orwell's madness and no idea about human suffering. But when it came to the game it was playing against B Corp, Alias trusted its ally. And when Albert–Calimero had asked the question *Can I win another golem?* the answer had been:

```
ydfnayes145788@qhjoify28jfao95j
e/vasyenfl/.65698aoi475f2jh
sfnayset20.docvjjzo818534j58/aiuyt
```

In the small hours, Albert received a visit from Orwell.

"Have you contacted Alias?"

"It's not that easy," Albert replied cautiously.

"If I brought you a finger or an ear belonging to Nadia Martin, would that stimulate your research?" Orwell made it sound like he was talking about a bottle of whisky or a box of cigars.

Albert knew Orwell was capable of cutting up Nadia, bit by bit. He gave in. "I've contacted Alias."

"Good, very good," said Orwell approvingly. "So can we design a new golem?"

Without answering, Albert returned to sequence 37 in his game and went inside the palace where the golem was waiting to be brought to life. He typed **EMET** and then clicked on a white blob that looked like a stain on the rug. Immediately the pile of pixels quivered. Slowly it shaped itself and took on the appearance of the podgy pasty golem. Then came the rattle of a typewriter and the following message appeared:

Enter your golem's name.

Albert looked at Orwell. "What shall I put?"

"B for Bernard, M for Martin and W for Webber..."

"BMW?"

As soon as the three letters had been entered, an identification sheet rolled down the screen.

> eye colour
> hair colour
> skin colour
> length and style of hair
> height
> weight

…and so on.

"What shall I put?" Albert asked wearily.

"If I give you the details of a real person, will the golem reproduce them?"

The question left Albert speechless. This was something he hadn't anticipated.

Orwell shoved a disk in front of him. "Yesterday, B Corp's board of directors went through a detection gate. Each person was scanned. I want my golem to look like Bernard Martin-Webber."

Albert shook his head, as if he considered the task impossible. But he inserted the disk. The different names appeared on the screen. Albert tried not to smile. All the directors had been scanned.

"Select BMW."

Albert did as he was told. Before his astonished eyes, the pasty golem was transformed into an executive in suit and tie. It was a faithful reproduction of the manager of Moreland Town Big B Stores, apart from one detail.

Orwell leant closer to the screen. "What's that on his forehead?"

"EMET," replied Albert calmly. "It's the trademark. Like *made in China*."

Orwell frowned. A scroll unfurled on the screen, with the following headings:

intelligence
character
special powers
skills

"He's stupid," said Orwell.

Albert gave the golem an IQ of eighty.

"He hasn't any special powers or skills," Orwell went on. "As for his character..." He hesitated for a fraction of a second. "Put *yoof and cool*."

By the end of the day, Golem BMW – stupid, yoof and cool – was ready for action. But what kind of action? Albert wondered, lying on his bunk.

As the night-time gloom filled his cell, he caught a glimmer of Orwell's monstrous project.

Swapping real people for golems.

The perfect crime.

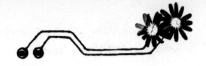

Iz What, This Mezz-Up?

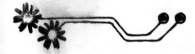

It wasn't until she started crying that Aisha realized how long she'd been bottling it all up. The tears that had been welling up inside her were spurting out now. And showing no signs of stopping.

The three boys stood around her. She didn't know whether to take Majid's or Sebastian's hand. So she grabbed Samir's T-shirt and sobbed against his chest.

The four beds lined up against the white wall looked like something out of a macabre fairy tale. The hospital room smelt like a prison.

Two days went by. Aisha cried in her sleep and

cried when she ate. Her eyes looked like two big red sponges. When Samir caught sight of Inspector Eberhardt, from the Swiss police, he called out loudly, "She's gotta get back to her place, you get me? Or her old man's gonna blast her."

"Don't worry," said Eberhardt. "Your parents have been informed."

"Why d'you tell them?" Samir objected. "They'll kill her twice over!"

The inspector gave the little girl from Mali a worried look. "We had to put your parents' minds at rest."

"My cousin Moussa, he went to Switzerland," sobbed Aisha. "And the police put him on a plane and sent him back to Bamako. But I want to go home. I don't want to go to Bamako."

The door opened. The woman who entered was wearing a long green dress and a veil. She came over to the children, but they couldn't actually see her walking. She seemed to be gliding across the floor. She had big blue eyes and longer incisors than Bugs Bunny.

"I'm Miss Goody," she said. "From the Red Cross."

"Miss Goody is an expert in victim support," the inspector added. "She's going to, er … support you."

Miss Goody immediately took both Aisha's hands and gave her a supportive smile so big, she felt she was being swallowed alive. Aisha wasn't scared any more. She was terrified.

"The inspector's going to ask you a few questions," Miss Goody explained. "But you don't have to answer if you don't want to. If there's a question that's bothering you, just give me a little sign. You could turn your thumb down, for example. This question bothers me, so I give the thumbs down! All right? Or, if you like, you can just answer with a simple nod or shake of the head."

"Do we get a wild card too?" Majid smirked.

The lady from the Red Cross let go of Aisha's hands and grabbed hold of Majid's. "Whatever you like, Majid. We're here to listen." She smiled for so long, Majid counted at least forty teeth.

Eberhardt cleared his throat. The Swiss police wanted to be nice to the kids, but they did have an investigation to carry out.

The interrogation was a ghastly ordeal for Majid, Samir, Aisha and Sebastian. Inspector Eberhardt would look back on it later as one of the most difficult moments in his career. He'd wanted to handle matters methodically, getting the children from Moreland Town to tell him about everything they'd been through since setting out from home. He'd been expecting the usual: merry-go-rounds and haunted houses, choo-choo trains and candyfloss. But he'd quickly found that he was losing control of the situation.

Not to put too fine a point on it, the kids were spouting a load of nonsense. Not only that, but they each gave a different version of events.

Fortunately, nothing phased Miss Goody.

"I think it's all got a little mixed up in your heads," she said cheerfully. "The characters at B Happy Land are just acts, you know that. They're a bit strange, but it's their job to entertain children. Sebastian, you're a sensible boy. You know B-Witched isn't a real witch, don't you?"

"Of course. She's Eddie, but he got hypnotized and…"

The inspector signalled to Miss Goody and drew

her aside. "Chances are these children have been drugged. They've lost all touch with reality."

Eberhardt didn't want the children's ravings to appear in their statements, because then they'd fall into the hands of the BIB boys. The inspector couldn't put his finger on why, but he didn't like the boys from the BIB. Not one little bit.

"Listen up, kids," he said. "You were supposed to have a great time at B Happy Land, but you got caught up in the middle of a terrorist operation. Witches and laser weapons are what you get in computer games. Real life isn't a computer game."

Eberhardt was glad to see Majid and Samir shaking their heads seriously. Maybe he'd managed to convince them. The hardest thing, he thought bitterly, is going to be convincing myself.

The next morning, Miss Goody accompanied the children to the airport and settled them into a small plane that had been specially chartered for them. On landing, they were going to be driven to another hospital for further examination.

On the plane, a glamorous air hostess gave them games, sweets and cartoons. In case the children still hadn't got over their adventure, she also made them swallow a blue pill. "It'll calm you down," she told them. Samir thanked her politely. But he'd seen so much medicine on Lulu's bedside table, pills that didn't do any good, he'd grown to hate them. He drank the glass of water and chucked the pill under his seat. He caught the air hostess's eye. If she'd seen him, she didn't say anything.

Ten minutes later she handed out headphones and switched on the miniature TV screens. A bit dazed by now, the children started watching cartoons. Bugs Bunny was on. Samir reckoned he was too old and killed the volume. He thought about Miss Goody, and turned to say something about her to Sebastian.

Which was when he noticed how stoned his neighbour looked. Sebastian was staring straight at the screen. Bugs Bunny had gone blurry. Geometric patterns kept appearing and disappearing before his eyes. Samir wanted to tell the air hostess. But then he noticed Majid and Aisha, on the other side of him, looking as dazed as Sebastian.

An endless black and white spiral was twirling on the screen. Samir felt dizzy and sick, so he looked away but turned up the volume. A stream of words was being crooned through the headphones, with music in the background. B Corp might have made mistakes, but it didn't want the lucky winners to have unhappy memories of their time at B Happy Land.

Listen to B Corp. Let B Corp tell you what to think…

When they got out of the ambulance, Samir immediately recognized Moreland Hospital where Lulu had been taken. The four children were separated. As soon as he was alone in his room, Samir tried the door handle.

"On the Koran of Mecca!"

He was locked in. Furiously he punched the door. Then he calmed down. He had to get out of here. He opened the window. No luck. He was on the third floor.

Suddenly the door opened and a girl from the catering team came in pushing a trolley. "Tea," she said. And off she went again.

Samir stayed still for a moment. The girl was bound to notice her mistake. He counted silently to ten before rushing towards the door.

Out in the corridor, he headed for the back staircase. He knew Lulu was on the fourth floor. On the stairs he passed a nurse, who gave him a surprised look. He was going to have to act fast. He burst out onto the fourth floor.

"Lulu!"

There she was, limp. The Force had left her.

Samir put his head on her pillow and whispered, "Lulu, you're not dead, are you? Lulu, it's me…"

"Samir?" came a tiny, disbelieving voice.

The two children stared at each other as if for the last time.

"Joke," murmured Lulu.

"I'm on my way."

Samir rushed straight back out again, bumping into a man in a white coat and dark glasses.

"Why don't you look where you're going, young man!" He grabbed Samir's T-shirt, but Samir went berserk trying to wriggle free, and the man with dark glasses lost his balance. "Hey, you, come back!"

Samir gave him the finger, before disappearing down the stairs.

The disused quarry wasn't far from the hospital. As he ran, Samir did a mental checklist of all the adults he'd come across lately: Natasha, Eddie, Orwell, Inspector Eberhardt, Miss Goody, the air hostess, the man with dark glasses. How could he tell goodies from baddies? All he knew was that he had to hurry if he wanted to save Lulu.

But when he got to the quarry he saw that somebody had beaten him to it. Somebody who'd parked their car there. Cautiously he made his way over. The car had a Swiss number plate. Even more alarming.

Samir ventured into a tunnel in search of Joke. In the gloom he could make out a sort of puddle that was glowing feebly. Joke was failing fast. Was he going to disappear altogether? Did electric ectoplasms die? And how was Samir going to feed him without any money?

He hit his forehead. "Duh!"

The car battery. Easy. He ran back to Joke with it. His generosity was immediately greeted with a resounding "Cock-a-doodle-doo! The sun's come out to play!" Followed by an ominous "Me still got munchies."

81

Alias

But with Joke taken care of for the time being, Samir started worrying about his own problems.

He'd have been even more worried if he'd seen the two armed men at the entrance to the quarry. He'd been followed. In a few seconds, the men from the Big Investigation Bureau would burst into action.

That same day, Mrs Badach went to pick up her son from Moreland Hospital. She'd been living on tenterhooks ever since the man from the Swiss police had called her. He'd told her about an "anti-globalization attack", and Emmay had asked him, "Iz what, this mezz-up?"

Apparently Inspector Eberhardt hadn't understood her question.

At the main entrance, Emmay saw Aisha's father and a distraught-looking couple, presumably Sebastian's parents. But she didn't get a chance to go over to them.

"Mrs Badach?"

She turned round. A man in a white coat and dark glasses asked again, "Are you Mrs Badach?"

"Yes, mister. You iz knowing where iz my

son?" She just wanted to take Majid home and pour him a glass of mint tea. After that, she'd see.

"Your son is still having a few problems adjusting to the real world," said the man by way of an answer. "Which is quite natural, given the trauma he's been through."

Emmay opened her mouth, then decided it was wiser to shut it again. "I can see him?" she asked gently.

"A meeting without an intermediary could prove detrimental." The man smiled thinly. Mrs Badach understood his smirk. He took her for an idiot.

"I'll show you to his room," continued the man, who hadn't even bothered to introduce himself.

In her head, Emmay called him Dark Glasses, and she didn't like Dark Glasses very much.

"Emmay!"

"Allah akbar!"

Mrs Badach barely had time to open her arms. Her last-born had never sought refuge in them like this before.

"Get me out of here. Let's go home," whispered Majid. "I haven't got my bag. I haven't got anything."

"Iz no big deal for your bag," said Emmay. "You iz alive. Iz more important." Taking her son by the hand, she walked towards the door. But Dark Glasses was blocking the way.

"Before you leave, I'd like Majid to tell you what happened to him."

"At home," exclaimed the young patient, who was starting to behave like a normal twelve-year-old again.

"No, *now*."

Mrs Badach shuddered slightly.

The man sensed he'd spoken too sharply and added, "Majid had a delirious episode on arrival here. I just want to check everything's back to normal. So, what happened to you, young man?"

Majid frowned, as if he was trying to piece together his memories. "We were in the car park at B Happy Land, the four of us, and we were about to get into Sebastian's camper van when, all of a sudden, two women ran into the car park."

He went quiet, as if he was trying to find the

right words. Actually, he was trying to find the pictures that went with the words.

"They opened fire on the workers from B Happy Land, who were dressed as cowboys, and then they told us to get inside the camper van."

Emmay was listening, agog. Majid went on to tell her how the two women had tied them up and driven them to Gruyères, where they'd blown up B Corp HQ. "But they were stopped by a police roadblock and they didn't get a chance to hold us hostage," Majid finished off.

"Good, very good," said Dark Glasses approvingly. Then he turned to Emmay. "It's quite possible your son's thoughts will drift again over the next few days. And he may even have a few panic attacks. So please make sure he takes these…" He held out two packets of blue pills. "Two, every evening. Three, if he's agitated."

Emmay nearly bowed as she took the medication. "Thank you, mister."

"In any case, a social worker will drop by to see how you're getting on. I'm assuming all your immigration papers are in order with the authorities?"

His tone was deceptively offhand. There was a

threat hanging in the air. Majid wasn't imagining it. "I was born here, you know," he said, trying to see the man's eyes behind all that dark glass.

The man put his hand on the doorknob. Before turning it, he added, "Ah yes, now this is very important, Mrs Badach. Majid mustn't see his friends for the time being."

"No way!" shouted Majid.

But Dark Glasses ignored him. "As I'm sure you'll appreciate, if they get together they'll only talk about what's happened. And that, in turn, will reactivate the trauma. I'm counting on you, Mrs Badach."

Emmay became even more docile and submissive. "Yes, mister."

The thin smile returned and Dark Glasses let Fatima and her son go through the door.

Out in the corridor, Majid's rantings were distinctly audible. "Oh my days, Emmay, don't tell me you're scared of him?"

"Shh!" said his mother, squeezing his hand. She didn't need to turn round to feel Dark Glasses' eyes on her back.

Mrs Badach put a plate of gazelle horns in front of her son. "So, you tell it me?" Free from Dark Glasses' clutches, she assumed her son would stop acting out this charade.

"But I've already told you!" Majid didn't want to talk about it again. Just thinking about it made him feel weirdly tired. He couldn't focus his thoughts.

"How they iz looking, the terrorists?"

Majid frowned. "Two women ran into the car park. They opened fire on the workers from B Happy Land, who—"

"Why you iz talking like that?" asked Emmay, sounding upset.

Majid looked around, at his computer on the table, the Babars on the wallpaper, the little decorated glass with mint tea steaming in it. He was back home now. But the alien feeling was still inside him.

"Two women ran into the car park," he whispered.

Nothing. He couldn't see anything. He couldn't describe the terrorists. He couldn't picture them. He gave his mother a despairing look.

"Iz no big deal," she clucked reassuringly. "Iz the trauma."

"Maybe I should take the pills?"

"Cakez iz more good," said Emmay, pushing the plate towards him.

Evening came. Majid dropped off the moment his head hit the pillow and Emmay stayed by his bedside for a while. Then she went into her own bedroom, a thousand muddled thoughts trapped inside her.

In the middle of the night, a scream made her sit bolt upright in bed.

"Emmay!"

She ran into Majid's room. Her son was sitting up and pointing, as he shouted, "Watch out, she's going to fire!" Then he covered his eyes with his hands and started sobbing. "Blood, there's so much blood…"

Gently Emmay shook him by the shoulder to bring him round.

"The pills," groaned Majid, "give me the pills."

Emmay switched the light on. She hesitated. There were no instructions on the packet.

"Give them to me, otherwise she'll come back."

"Who?"

"The terrorist."

"You iz seeing her in your dream? How she iz?"

"Two women ran into the car park," Majid muttered.

"That iz not dream. Iz lesson."

Majid didn't answer. He was racking his brain, trying to find the pictures from his dream. A woman. Holding a gun. She fires. There's blood on the bedcover. But it all got blurred and that haunting phrase took over.

Two women ran into the car park.

The social worker showed up at nine o'clock the next morning.

"Everything all right, Mrs Badach?"

Emmay knew the social workers who dealt with Hummingbird Tower. And this woman wasn't one of them. "Yes, missus, thank you."

The social worker went through into the living room, where she saw Majid. "So, has Majid been taking his medicine?"

Majid, who was still half asleep, grunted. The social worker put a fresh packet on the table. "The doctor forgot to prescribe these. One in the morning and one at midday, in addition to the blue pills in the evening."

Emmay nodded, pretending to be dim. Suddenly the woman was standing in front of her.

"Isn't your husband around, Mrs Badach?"

"Iz his new job. Iz lorries."

"A lorry driver? And all your papers and work permits are in order? Because that certainly wasn't the case round at your neighbours'…"

Emmay understood. Aisha's parents had already had their visit.

"You iz wanting to see papers?"

"No, I'll take your word for it. But I know your son Haziz has had a few run-ins with the law. We don't want you drawing attention to yourselves, now do we?"

Emmay came over all scared and started moaning. "My poor Haziz, iz not his fault. Iz bad luck. You like glass of tea, or a cake? Littel cakez for childrin, innit?"

After thrusting some very sticky cakes into her hands, Emmay accompanied the woman to the front door. Then she went back into the living room, grabbed the packet of pills lying on the table and threw it into the kitchen bin.

Majid was amazed. "What are you doing?"

"Iz not social worker," she said. "Iz big fat liar. And Dark Glasses, iz not doctor, iz..." Emmay, who wanted to play that man at his own pretentious game, concluded firmly, "Iz psychopath."

Sorry

The men from the BIB were in the quarry. They'd watched Samir steal the battery and disappear into the tunnel.

Tommy had taken charge. "Stay here!"

Payne crouched down behind the car. Tommy slid a hand inside his jacket for his gun. Then he headed into the tunnel, sweeping the area with his revolver.

Suddenly a supernatural voice made him glue himself to the sweaty wall. "Yippee-yay! It's pa-aa-arty time!"

It can talk, thought Tommy, scowling. But what was it saying?

"Kisses, friend."

Ten years of working for the BIB might have prepared Tommy for an encounter of the third kind. But it didn't lessen the shock. The thing was sparking and making a ridiculous attempt to look like a human being. It was trying to lure its victims by repeating, "Stroke me. Me friend."

Tommy took this to mean the creature had spotted him, and he started firing. Cries of panic filled the tunnel. But it wasn't the creature. It was the kid. Tommy had nearly killed him.

"Walk towards me!" he shouted to Samir. "I'll cover you."

Samir crawled over to the BIB director of operations, who grabbed him and pushed him to safety, almost knocking him out against the wall.

"Is this a film or something?" stammered Samir.

"Don't be frightened," said Tommy. "The thing can't do anything to hurt you. I'm here now."

Joke giggled. "Yippee-yay! It's pa-aa-arty time!"

Tommy muttered two or three unrepeatable words: the kind you'd hear in an uncut version of Puff Z Sniddy. Then he twisted Samir's wrist, forcing him away down the tunnel.

Back in the main dugout they were greeted with a thunderous *"Hands up!"* Payne had his finger on the trigger. When he recognized his colleague, he re-holstered his gun.

"They're down there," said Tommy, pointing at the entrance to the tunnel.

"You saw them?"

Tommy blinked. "I saved the kid."

Samir was rubbing the top of his head. Payne turned to him. "D'you know how many there are?"

"Er … one."

Payne gave a grim smile. Poor kid. No idea…

"It's a nest, d'you understand? There must be hundreds of them in these tunnels."

Samir's eyes bulged. Hundreds of Jokes?

"They're invading us," Tommy explained. "They don't have a shape of their own. They have to invade human bodies. Have you heard of Natasha?"

Samir pulled a face.

"She was just a normal young woman," said Payne. "She wanted to love and be loved. Now she's possessed by one of these ectoplasms."

The word *ectoplasm* made Samir shudder. Did these two Americans know something he didn't?

Tommy questioned him again. "Do you know any other people, like Natasha, who've suddenly started behaving differently?"

"Er, well, there's Lulu. She's my kid sister. She's connected to Joke's megawave. I mean, you know, it's a kind of—"

"And where's your little sister now?" asked Payne, trying to sound friendly.

"Banged up in Moreland Hospital."

Dark Glasses was surprised to see Samir back again with Payne. It was on the BIB's orders that he'd let the kid out. "Everything all right?"

"A1," Payne assured him. "Seal off the fourth floor. Clear the area."

Samir was more impressed by the minute.

"I've just spoken to the nurses," Payne told him. "Your sister's got a disease that zaps her strength. Now, all of a sudden, she's full of beans. This monster thing, what d'you call it again?"

"Joke."

"This monster ... this Joke ... it's trying to possess your sister. By *remote access*. D'you realize what that means? Have you any idea?"

Samir's head was spinning.

"If it succeeds, it'll turn her into another Natasha. A murderer. We've got to avoid that at all costs. Are you ready to help?"

Samir was paralysed with fear. Payne gave him a friendly punch. "We're going to do a swell job together, you and me, buddy."

Samir was kept in solitary confinement for an hour in the nurses' off-duty room. Then they took him to Lulu.

"Samir!" she shouted, stretching out her arms.

The little girl's head was encased in a kind of helmet, and giant plasters with a rainbow of tubes sticking out of them covered her arms and chest.

"What is this? A sci-fi lab?" He was outraged.

The room was full of screens with white lines that dipped and rose, dots that jumped about, flashing red lights. Everything was bleeping. Despite being injected with a sedative, Lulu was still very agitated. She'd already ripped out the tubes linking her to the machines three times. According to Payne, this proved that Joke the ectoplasm was trying to take possession of her.

As soon as Samir sat down beside her, Lulu relaxed. "He's … he's not going to hurt you," her big brother stammered. "He's like a doctor." He was pointing at Payne.

"And look, I'm wearing a helmet too," said Payne, grinning. "Hey, earth calling Mars, can you hear me?"

Nobody laughed.

"Right, OK," he said to Samir, "keep her busy. Tell her a story."

Samir gave Payne a mean look. He could tell the BIB guy was using him, even if he made out he was being friendly. He grabbed the furry koala lying on his little sister's bed and, glumly, started telling the story of Koko, the koala that walked upside down because he came from Australia. He made Koko bounce around on his head. *Boing, boing!* Lulu smiled faintly.

Payne lost interest in the children and turned to adjust his headphones. "*One, two, three. One, two, three, Tommy?*"

Tommy looked like an astronaut, all geared up in a jumpsuit and a helmet with a perspex visor.

The outfit offered reasonable protection, but didn't score when it came to comfort. He was far too hot, and each time he opened his mouth to speak or breathe, the perspex fogged up.

The dugout looked like it was being made ready for another games tournament. Control panels, computers, measuring equipment, generators: Tommy had unloaded the whole lot in an hour. And that wasn't counting the reservoir of pressurized water. Wisely, he had started by increasing the water supply to the pool at the tunnel entrance. If what Samir said was anything to go by, the creature was more scared of water than anything else.

When Payne gave him the signal from the hospital room, Tommy switched on his equipment. He was gobsmacked by how quickly the creature reacted. Joke appeared from his hideout like a moth attracted to light.

"What a monster!" Tommy whispered inside his helmet. He took a deep breath and, without taking his eyes off the monster, picked up his submachine gun. It didn't weigh much. He'd bought it from Big B Stores. Toy section.

"Phase one," he muttered, then aimed at the ectoplasm and let rip. A storm of ping-pong balls rained down on the lumpish body with its hazy outline. They disappeared in a series of sparks. Confirming the creature's destructive powers.

Back at the hospital, Payne was listening intently to his colleague through his headphones as Samir made up stories about Bottom-Burper Koko, the koala that always had his bum in the air.

Suddenly he turned to the children, interrupting them sharply. "Tommy says Joke said 'Cock-a-doodle-doo!' D'you understand the meaning of that phrase?"

"It's because of the Furby," Samir explained.

"Because of *what*?"

"It's because he swallowed a... He's talking in Furby-speak," said Samir, cutting a long story short. "That's his language."

"And do you kids know how to talk in Furby-speak?"

"Kind of," Samir confessed. "Mostly Lulu."

"Ah... Could Lulu say something to me in Furby-speak?"

Lulu thought about it as she stared at the ceiling, and then said in a robotic voice, "Me still sleepy."

Taken aback, Payne relayed the sentence to his colleague.

A moment later, Tommy declared, "Communication established. Ectoplasm does indeed appear to converse in Furby-speak. Has responded with 'Stroke me.' Meaning unknown."

A short while later, he added, "Ready for phase two. Storm of metallic objects."

Tommy repeated the ping-pong ball experiment, this time using nuts and bolts from the hardware section at Big B Stores. The small metallic pieces produced flashes and mini-explosions when they came into contact with the monster. He checked the screen of his spectroscopic device. Undeniably, terrifyingly, there was the result.

"Tommy here. Analysis completed. The creature is composed of pure energy. I repeat: the creature is composed of pure energy."

Back in Lulu's room, Payne scowled. For the last few hours, he'd been thinking of running away with the monster. Taking it back with them, like that moment when King Kong arrives in New York in chains. But pure energy ... now that didn't sound easy to chain down. Best to destroy it, particularly since the little girl was becoming increasingly agitated.

In fact, Lulu was laughing because Samir was getting carried away with the story of Krappy Koko, the koala that made a stinky mess all over the sheets.

"Let's proceed to the laser phase," Payne ordered his colleague.

"Message received."

The laser beam shot out of a kind of cannon and hit Joke bang on target. The effect was immediate and spectacular. Everything fizzed on the spectroscope screen, as if Joke had been thrown into a particle accelerator. But the creature didn't seem to mind. In fact, it looked like it was becoming even more solid. And bigger.

"You'd think the laser was feeding it," he told his colleague from the BIB.

Which Joke then confirmed with a loud "Me still got munchies!"

Furby-speak wasn't that difficult to understand after all.

Lulu was laughing hysterically. She wanted to get up, jump about, dance.

"Hold her tight!" Payne shouted to Samir. "She mustn't pull out the wires."

Samir was more interested in what was happening on the screens. He could see the white lines surging in peaks and troughs, the markers picking up speed, the flashes going crazy.

The strange creature was trying to slip its electric being inside the body of a child weakened by disease. In the olden days it would have been called witchcraft. A case of demonic possession.

Suddenly all the indicator lights exploded. The white lines froze. The measuring equipment sparked. Samir shrieked and was flung backwards as Lulu leapt to her feet and started jumping on the bed like it was a trampoline. Higher and higher, with insane energy. On the third jump, her hair brushed the ceiling.

"Stop!" Payne roared into his receiver. "Stop! Stop right now!"

But there was no reply. The connection had been broken.

"Oh my God! No! No!" Tommy's voice echoed inside his helmet.

Joke had swollen up out of all proportion. But that wasn't the worst of it. The creature was floating in mid-air, like a hot-air balloon. And it looked to Tommy like it was heading straight for him.

Then he realized. The creature wasn't floating. It was climbing back up the laser beam towards its source, a luminous tightrope walker balancing on a line of energy.

Tommy rushed over to the beam-emitting cannon and pressed the interrupter to cut off the flow.

For a brief moment, Joke was suspended under the arched roof of the dugout. Then he came crashing down into the dark pool of water. A host of little bubbles rose to the surface, as if he was expelling air. But Joke was made of pure energy. He didn't have any lungs to empty. The pool was, quite simply, starting to boil.

And the electric ectoplasm couldn't reassemble itself in water.

In the hospital room, somewhere between the bed and the ceiling, Lulu suddenly spread her arms, as if she'd been hit in the chest. Then she collapsed onto the mattress, floppy as a rag doll.

The Force had just been wrenched away from her for ever.

"Joke!" she cried out. "Joke, don't be dead."

"Lulu! Lulu!" bellowed Samir. He shook her, slapped her. Her lips were white, her skin almost grey. She wasn't responding.

"What have you done to her?" he moaned. "You've killed her! My little sister. My kid... She's all I've got, all I've got ... and you've gone and killed her."

"Sorry," said Payne.

That evening, Orwell didn't understand a single word of the fax that came through from the BIB.

We've destroyed the thing. There weren't any more in the quarry. Once again, the Big Investigation Bureau has warded off the invasion. We regret we couldn't save the child.

He scrunched the fax into a ball, muttering, "Bunch of morons." They hadn't even managed to track down Natasha. But then he remembered he still had

Albert at his mercy, and he calmed down. The young computer programmer would do whatever Orwell told him, as long as he feared for Nadia Martin's life.

And on that front we're sorted, thought Orwell.

Because Nadia Martin's life was in the hands of Miss Goody.

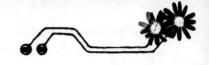

Totally Loopy

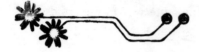

Free! Nothing could be bleaker than this bare room with just an old black and white photo of the Alps for decoration. Nothing could be less cheerful than the smells of ether and bleach. But at least there were no bars at the window. And no guards behind the door.

Nadia was free. Or nearly. First, she had to recover. A few days of rest. A few pills. Quite a lot of pills, actually. Two little bitter blue ones in the morning. A big yellow lemon-flavoured one at midday. A red and green capsule with her cup of tea at four o'clock. And two more bitter pills in the evening. They put drops in her glass of water and powder in her yogurt. For her own good.

Nadia was told she'd been through a horrific ordeal. If she was sensible and took her medication, she wouldn't have any more panic attacks, she'd be in a good mood again, she'd stop feeling so tired. Everything would work out fine. The nurses never mentioned the word *hospital*. They referred to it as the sanctuary.

"Swallow that for me."

"Now the yellow one."

"There we go! Twelve drops."

"Still feeling a little bit tired? That's normal. The doctor said that's *perfectly* normal."

Nadia kept swallowing. She felt even more tired. As far as she was concerned, things were getting less and less normal. By the time she'd started to understand, she no longer had the strength to react.

There are prisons with bars and prisons without bars. It wasn't her body they wanted to keep in a cage. It was her mind.

A nurse leant over her. For once, she wasn't holding out a tablet and a glass of water. "You've got a visitor," she announced.

Nadia's heart started thumping. Who? Who was coming? She struggled against the haze floating before her eyes. She wanted to see who was going to walk in. She needed to hug somebody so badly. Oh, Albert...

Propped up weakly on her pillows, she watched the door.

It was a woman. Somebody Nadia didn't know. She was wearing a long green dress and a veil, like a nun or an old-fashioned nurse. When she smiled, she flashed two rows of gigantic teeth. She smiled all the time.

Miss Goody said she worked for the Red Cross. She wanted to help Nadia. And talking was the best cure.

"You've got to get it out of your head. You've had some very difficult experiences. You need to let go. So tell me everything that happened, everything you can remember. I'm here to listen and help you get it all out. You'll feel better afterwards. All right, Nadia?"

Nadia nodded.

But talking was hard. It felt like a concrete slab was weighing down her tongue.

"Too much medication. As soon as you're on the mend, the doctor will reduce the dose."

Miss Goody came once in the morning and once in the afternoon. She asked short questions, gently. Then she listened. She let Nadia talk.

Nadia was having a dreadful time trying to order her thoughts. A car park duel between cowboys and a Lara Croft lookalike shooting beams from an eraser-laser. A child dying and coming back to life. The best-defended bunker in the world besieged by two scantily clad young women. A portcullis nailing men to the ground. The boss of the all-powerful Big B Corporation with a bullet in his head. B Corp HQ getting blown up.

Was it really just the two of us? Me and Natasha? Did we bring down the most powerful private organization on the planet?

Help… It doesn't make sense!

But that's what I remember. I know that's what I remember. If it's a lie, I've gone loopy.

And that was exactly what Nadia read in Miss Goody's attentive eyes, behind her unchanging smile. You poor thing, you're totally loopy.

All the same, Miss Goody appeared satisfied.

To Nadia's great surprise, she declared, "Well done, we've made excellent progress. Things are slowly falling back into place again in your head. I think you've earned a treat. Aren't you starting to get a bit bored?"

Miss Goody promised they'd have a walk in the grounds soon. "And look, Nadia, I've brought you a present."

A blue nightie. Brand new. Nadia thanked her.

In preparation for her walk, she forced herself to move around her room. From the bed to the wall, the wall to the door, the door to the window. She hadn't felt so tired these last couple of days. Her legs were stronger. But she didn't let it show.

Because there was a reason for her renewed energy, and she was terrified of being found out. She kept the tablets under her tongue and spat them out again as soon as the nurse had turned away. The fewer pills Nadia swallowed, the more her strength started to come back. Unfortunately her brain cells were taking much longer to tone up than her muscles.

She'd been in the bathroom, holding the blue nightie, when she'd decided she had to do something. She'd been about to try it on when she'd noticed the label. *Beautiful B*. Did Fit B's girlfriend have a line of clothes too? She'd imagined the pair of them sitting on a Big B sofa, watching their BIT digital TV. Two soulless beings. Two robots.

Albert, help, I've got a heart. I love you!

The tears had rolled down her cheeks. She'd pressed the foot pedal on the little white bin to chuck the nightie. It'd been nearly full. She'd bent down and found it crammed with medication boxes. She didn't want to know what they were. She didn't want to know what she'd been swallowing for days. She'd seen just one thing on each box, on each tube: BIG B LABORATORIES.

Nadia had started tearing the nightie into long strips. Miss Goody wouldn't approve, but she didn't care. Because Miss Goody was the same brand as the Beautiful B nightie, the BIT digital TV, the Big B Laboratories medicine, the Big Smile toothpaste and the B Silky sheets.

Miss Goody was another B Corp product.

It was hot. Out of her window, Nadia could see the grounds flooded in bright sunshine.

"So, what about our stroll?" asked Miss Goody, flashing her dazzling teeth that were brushed with Big Smile toothpaste. "Are you ready?"

Nadia nodded. "You'll have to help me," she said, sitting up in bed.

"Of course, my child. Take my arm."

Nadia held on to Miss Goody's right wrist. Gripping it hard, she hauled herself up out of bed. She was standing now but she didn't let go of Miss Goody's wrist.

"Nadia? What are you doing?"

What was she doing? She was twisting Miss Goody's arm ... slowly ... still holding that wrist firmly, and raising it behind Miss Goody's back.

"Nadia, don't! Na—" Miss Goody stopped talking when she felt her hand level with her shoulder blade. She was paralysed with shock.

"Sometimes it's the shoulder that gives way, and sometimes it's the arm that bweaks," said Nadia. "Which would you pwefer?"

"You're mad!"

"Yes. Totally loopy."

Miss Goody made a supreme effort to recover her jovial smile and cheerful tone of voice. "Look, let's talk," she suggested. "I'll do anything to help you, Nadia, you know that."

"I know who you are. You're from B Corp."

"From where?"

Nadia gave a little tug and the Red Cross representative let out a cry of pain.

"I think the arm's going to bweak first. The bone doesn't seem very stwong." She made her victim kneel down on the edge of the bed. "Do what I tell you. Pull back the sheet, to the wight of the pillow."

Miss Goody did as she was told. Under the sheet were fifteen blue pills and some red and green capsules.

"Take them," ordered Nadia, "and swallow the whole lot."

"That's ridiculous! Nadia, come on... Ouch!"

"Hurry up!" Nadia exerted more pressure on Miss Goody's arm.

"It's dangerous. I can't swallow all those pills."

"I'm cwazy, Miss Goody. And when I have an attack, I love bweaking arms. Go on! Hurry up!

You'll have to excuse me, I've alweady sucked them a bit."

Miss Goody was fond of her right arm. With her left hand, she grabbed a few pills and swallowed them.

"And again," said Nadia. "There's a glass of water on the locker."

When all the pills and all the capsules had disappeared, Nadia took the shredded nightie out of her dressing-gown pocket. "Open your mouth," she ordered. "Don't worry, I won't make you swallow this time."

Nadia made Miss Goody lie down on the bed, and she tied her hands behind her back. Then she waited. She knew nobody ever came into her room while the lady from the Red Cross was visiting.

The drugs took more than half an hour to work. Once Miss Goody was asleep, Nadia untied her hands and started undressing her. Then she rummaged around in her visitor's little black bag and took out all the money she could find.

A few minutes later, she left the room, wearing a veil and a dress that was too long for her.

"Goodbye, Miss Goody."

Nadia nodded at the nurse standing in the staffroom doorway, watching her walk down the corridor. Pulling the veil down firmly, she carried on until she reached the stairs. There was only one floor, she knew that. She quickened her step once she'd got past reception and made her way across the grounds. She went through a metal gate and found herself on a country road.

Nadia didn't know where she was. Not only that, but her legs weren't going to hold out much longer. So she positioned herself near a junction and stuck out her thumb.

Two lorries and a dozen cars went past without slowing down. The red car looked like it was going to do the same, but the driver must have felt a pang of guilt, because he braked and reversed.

Nadia blinked. This *had* to be a bad joke.

The red car was a convertible. The door swung open to reveal a man in his thirties, with a long nose and eyes that were too close together. Stefano! The playboy who'd denounced her as a terrorist.

"Get in, Sister."

It was too late to escape. Nadia got in, checking that the veil was covering her face.

"Where are you going?"

Nadia searched for the right words. She had to disguise her voice, of course. Above all, she mustn't give herself away by lisping. "To ... to the next town."

"Lausanne?"

"Yes."

Stefano chuckled. "I'd vowed never to pick up hitch-hikers ever again. Especially female hitchers! But I reckon I can make an exception for nuns. Not much risk there, hey?"

"No."

Stefano drove in silence for a minute. "D'you want to know why? I mean, why I don't pick up women hitch-hikers any more?"

"Yes," said Nadia, so quietly he could barely hear her.

"You'll never believe me if I tell you. But I swear it's the honest truth!"

"You mustn't swear, my son."

"Sorry, Sister. Well, here goes. The other day, I see two babes – two young women – on the road to Gruyères. One of them's drop-dead gorgeous with massive... Very pretty, you get the picture."

"And the other?" asked Nadia, curious.

"Oh, you know, not bad-looking. But kind of uptight. Serious."

Nadia was irritated. "Don't you like sewious young women, my son?" She bit her lip, but he hadn't noticed.

"No – I mean, yes! But wait till you hear what happened next. I could tell straight off there was something weird about these girls…"

Nadia listened to Stefano's account with growing relief. I'm not mad, she thought. What I remember actually happened.

"And there you have it," he finished. "I stumbled on two terrorists and now I keep having nightmares. I've aged twenty years, just like that. But why did it happen to me, hey? Why me? Can your God answer that, Sister?"

Time for her revenge. "It's to give your life more meaning, my son. You see, sex without love is like a convertible without the woof down."

Stefano's eyebrows shot up. He was speechless. Then, perhaps because he was already on the path to repentance, he made a detour to drop Nadia off at the train station.

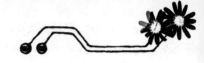

Love Conquers All

Mrs Mullins had reacted just as Emmay would have done in the same situation. She'd put the kettle on. Samir was sitting on a chair in the kitchen. He kept rubbing his face and running his fingers through his hair, but it didn't seem to help. He'd already told Hugh and his mother his story twice over.

"Guys with guns, you get me, from the BIB? They made it so I couldn't think straight, and I helped them kill my sister." He sniffed and rubbed his face again, hard.

"Is she in a coma?" Hugh wanted to know.

"Yeah. She can't even breathe by herself any more."

Samir started crying again, even though he'd been trying really hard not to. He could still hear Lulu's laughter from when they were playing with Koala. "I think they're going to switch her off. The doctor with the dark glasses wants to get rid of her, I swear. And there's nobody to protect her." He pointed to himself, as if he didn't count for anything. "Nobody."

"That's outrageous!" objected Mrs Mullins. "I'll go over there, Samir…" She fell silent. Natasha had appeared in the doorway.

Samir let out a scared yelp. He hadn't seen the girl-golem since that night in the bunker. "She … she's here," he stammered. "Does her weapon thing still work?"

The eraser-laser was slung over Natasha's shoulder, switched off.

"Don't worry, she won't hurt you," said Hugh. He turned to Natasha. "This is Samir. Samir is an ally."

"Samir has water on his face," Natasha observed.

Lulu's big brother wiped his cheeks with the back of his hand.

"They're tears," said Hugh. "Samir is crying."

"Hugh cries too," Natasha remembered.

The young teacher blushed. "Yeah, it happens sometimes. When I'm sad."

"Samir is sad," she deduced.

Hugh glanced at her admiringly. "You see, Mum? See how quickly she can work things out now."

"Yes, dear," agreed Mrs Mullins, who couldn't help thinking a three-year-old would have done as much.

"Why is Samir sad?" asked Natasha, sounding just like the three-year-old in question.

"Joke's dead," explained Samir. "He was connected to my sister. And now Lulu hasn't got the Force any more. She's going to die."

"Lulu, number of lives remaining: zero," Natasha recited.

"Wow, she's *totally* following what we're saying," Hugh exclaimed.

His mother gave him an exasperated look. But Samir was starting to see Natasha in a different light. "Tell me, er…"

"Natasha," Hugh whispered.

"Natasha," said Samir, plucking up courage.

"D'you think ... could Joke come out of the computer again?"

"Alias is my master," Natasha told him. "Alias decides."

"But we can't contact Alias," said Hugh. No sooner were the words out of his mouth than he realized his mistake. Alias *could* be contacted. But he had no intention of saying how.

"I am going to transfer the data," Natasha decided.

Hugh was blown away. Natasha's powers of reasoning were far greater than he'd realized.

"Mother-Ally," she said, "give me some water."

"Don't listen to her," panicked Hugh.

"But it's a fantastic idea!" marvelled Mrs Mullins. "Natasha can go back inside the computer and ask Alias to let Joke out again."

Hugh thumped the table, making the cups and saucers jiggle. "No way. Natasha's only got two lives left."

"And what about Lulu?" Samir shouted. "She's got zero!"

Mrs Mullins quickly took control. She congratulated Natasha for offering to sacrifice one of her lives to save Lulu. Then she turned to Hugh, who was vehemently shaking his head.

"No, no way. I don't want her to. It means her going back to B Corp. I won't have it."

Mrs Mullins gave her son an aggrieved look. A virtual being mattered to him more than a little girl.

While the grown-ups were busy arguing, Samir grabbed the kettle Mrs Mullins had put on to make the tea. He set it down gently on the table and flipped open the lid. Natasha was watching him. He cupped his hands in a begging gesture. Before Hugh could stop her, the girl-golem had stuck her hand in the water.

She let out a cry of surprise and then gave the following analysis: "Invincible armour operational at eighty per cent."

Hugh had won invincible armour for her in the game. It hadn't worked until now.

But Natasha was making strange whimpering noises. She held out her wet hand to Hugh. Her skin had gone red. "ALT F4," she said, looking panicky. "ALT F4."

Hugh took her hand. She'd scalded herself. At last she was finding out what pain meant. "Does it hurt?"

"Stop hurt," she begged.

"Run some cold water on it," Mrs Mullins advised, turning on the tap.

"Invincible armour operational at seventy per cent," Natasha analysed.

Hugh turned the tap off fast. Natasha appeared to be losing her protection.

"A lot of water required to kill Natasha," said the girl-golem.

"Why don't we just fill up the bath?" Samir suggested.

"I refuse ... I forbid..." Hugh spluttered. "I ... I love Natasha and nobody has the right to..." He went quiet, ashamed, and turned to Natasha for support.

She echoed his declaration. "Natasha loves Hugh."

He smiled, relieved. She loved him, so she'd stay.

"But Natasha will save the girl-human," she added.

Silence descended on the kitchen. The virtual being had just given Hugh a lesson in humanity.

"Natasha is sad," she whispered.

"She's amazing!" exclaimed Mrs Mullins, won over at last.

Hugh realized he had to prove himself worthy of her love. "Come on," he said to Natasha.

He took her hand and they went into the bathroom together.

They watched the water running. In a few seconds, they'd be separated. Hugh leant against the locked door. With his head lolling gently backwards and a faraway look in his eyes, he let his heart do the talking.

"Natasha, before you … go, I want to ask your forgiveness. When I created you, I was just a stupid bloke. All I wanted was a blonde with big boobs." He tried to laugh but his tears were choking him. "I didn't know I would really love you. You are … you're my first love."

He looked at her. How was she meant to understand the way he felt? He hardly did.

The water level was rising. He dipped his hand

in to check the temperature. Not too hot, not too cold. At least she wouldn't suffer. He felt he was making a sacrifice to a barbaric god called Alias.

"There we go," he said, turning off the taps.

Natasha placed a finger on Hugh's lips. It was her way of asking him. He hugged her, kissed her and then pushed her away gently. "Save Lulu." He felt like he was about to faint.

Natasha put her hands to her heart. "Hurt."

They loved each other, the gamer and his she-warrior.

Natasha stepped into the tub. The water reached her knees. She shuddered, and clutched herself. "Invincible armour operational at thirty per cent…"

Slowly she crouched down.

"Twenty per cent … fifteen per cent…"

She looked at Hugh, fear and refusal in her eyes. "No!" she cried.

There was an explosion.

Then nothing.

Hugh slid down the door until his head hit the tiled floor.

"Natasha," he whispered, one last time.

A BMW? No Problem...

After two days and two nights in his cell, Albert was happy to be in BMW's office in Moreland Town Big B Stores. Hands in his pockets, he looked around sneeringly. The cashiers' roll of honour featured a photograph of Soraya, this year's top cashier. The slogans on the paper banners read: *Selling is Living* and *A good trolley is a full trolley*.

"That's priceless, that is," he said, looking at one which read: *An aisle without special offers is like a wig with no hair*.

"I didn't bring you here to make fun of the management style in my stores," Orwell commented icily from behind him.

Albert had got his way. He'd managed to convince Orwell to move the electric blue computer, which was now on Bernard Martin-Webber's desk.

As he'd explained to Orwell, creating a golem was one thing, recalling it was another. Once the golem came out of the computer, there was a risk they might lose control over it. Since the experiment involved observing the behaviour of a second BMW, they needed to take it to the manager's natural habitat.

Orwell was suspicious of Albert and everything he said. So he'd taken certain precautions. There were three armed men prowling the shop floor.

At this precise moment, the real BMW was basking in unaccustomed glory.

Life's certainly taken a turn for the better, he thought. Now I'm a member of the board of directors, it's a whole different story!

He was being driven through the heart of the city in a black limousine, by a chauffeur with a peaked cap. There was a train ticket in his pocket. First class, of course. His destination: Rotten-Sodbury. His mission: a feasibility study on buying up (for peanuts) the old Toolinex industrial premises. The plan: to build a Big B super-complex, comprising a Big B Stores, a B Max cinema and a Big Burger outlet.

But something was bugging him.

"D'you often drive directors?" he asked the chauffeur.

"Yes, sir."

"And do they often go to places like Rotten-Sodbury?"

"Never, sir."

I thought as much, reflected BMW. This assignment isn't director level. It must be because I'm new...

"Shall I drop you off here, sir?"

The limo had stopped in front of the station. It was on the tip of BMW's tongue to ask the chauffeur if it wasn't customary for him to accompany directors all the way to the platform, carrying their briefcase for them.

"Yes, that's fine," he muttered.

As he was getting out of the limo, BMW realized nobody had said anything about his return journey. Would he be picked up? Highly unlikely. At the end of the day, he brooded, my life hasn't changed that much.

Inside the station, he caught sight of the electronic display: DELAYS OCCURRING. A tinny voice confirmed this information: "Following a strike by railway workers, major delays are expected…"

Shaking his head, BMW made his way to platform eight.

Two banners greeted him. One said: *We want a 32-hour week, and we want it now!* The other announced: *Railway workers in support of Toolinex workers.*

He swore. No chance of getting to Rotten-Sodbury. And, of course, the chauffeur had dropped him off in a hurry.

Knowing his luck, the Moreland Light Railway workers would be on strike too.

The BMW stamping his feet on platform eight thought he was one of a kind. But just a few miles away, a creature with identical features was smiling on the screen of the electric blue computer.

For once, Albert felt a connection with Orwell. They shared the same curiosity, the same desire to succeed. He didn't like having something in common with the head of B Corp. But he was caught up in the excitement of the moment. He – yes, he – was going to make a golem come out of the magic box.

When a fine grid pattern covered the outline of the golem and a beam of light suddenly shot out from the screen, Albert felt a rush of pride. Golem was his game and the computer belonged to him.

Close by, Orwell was brandishing a ridiculous transparent pistol. A kid's toy which he'd filled with water. "It works," he whispered. "It works!" The water pistol wobbled.

The computer was making whirring noises. Gradually the criss-cross pattern faded and the shape become more solid. Soon the hologram floating above the floor was transformed into a convincing version of the manager, his feet firmly on the carpet.

There was just one problem. On his exposed forehead, four letters stood out: EMET.

"That's all people are going to see," complained Orwell. "Give it the cap."

Albert threw a Big B Stores cap to the golem, who caught it neatly.

"Put the cap on," Albert ordered, the same way he'd have said "Down, boy!" to his dog.

"Heavy, man!" exclaimed BMW 2, jamming the cap onto his head.

"No!" shouted Orwell. "Not like that."

The golem had put the cap on back to front, yoof style. "Take it easy, man!" BMW commented breezily. He grinned fatuously, revealing Big Smile sparkling teeth. Then he put his hand on the door-knob, as if intending to head off. Orwell stayed calm. He knew the door was locked. But BMW passed straight through it, dissipating into billions of pixels.

"Nuff respect!" he said from the other side.

Orwell gave Albert a panicked look. "Did you know about that? How come he can go through walls?"

Albert laughed out loud. "Great, isn't it?"

"Moron," muttered Orwell.

It was a Wednesday morning and the store was quiet. A few kids were eyeing up packets of Big Munchie bars (a new product that hadn't really caught on yet) and egging each other on to steal them.

"Aargh, man! It's the manager!" one of them called out.

BMW had appeared out of nowhere, all smile and branded forehead. "Hey, brethren!" he said. "Respect for your manager's cool headgear!"

The kids stood there, agog.

"Let's big it up for the main man at Wide Boy Stores!" the golem persisted. Then he tried a different tack. "How about some farting goo?"

The kids backed off as if they'd just seen the devil.

"Farting goo's evil, man."

"FG's banned."

A little further off, in the household section, a large lady in a shawl was comparing prices with a calculator in her hand. The real BMW would have recognized Mrs Goldberg, who'd been scandalously eliminated from the dream weekend to B Happy Land competition. But his golem sidled happily up to her.

"How about some farting goo?"

Mrs Goldberg gave him an indignant look and murmured, "The man's deranged."

Which triggered the inevitable "Let's big it up for the main man!"

Mrs Goldberg pulled her shawl up tightly to her chin. "He's a pervert," she whispered, moving away. "A dirty old man."

"Yoof, more like!" the golem protested.

In the fresh produce aisle, a young employee was talking enthusiastically into a mike about French artichokes. "Don't miss our fresh produce of the day," she was saying. "Are artichokes better served hot or cold? The choice is yours, but hurry, because they're only on special offer for another half-hour. Ah, I've just spotted our manager, who's bound to have a new special off—"

The sales assistant broke off but her mouth stayed wide open. She'd just seen the four letters stamped on the golem's forehead. Wiping her own forehead with the back of her hand, she signalled to him to do likewise.

But BMW went right up to her and crooned into the mike, "How about some farting goo?"

Albert and Orwell were following the golem's movements on the monitors used by the real BMW to keep an eye on his customers.

"He just needs a bit of fine-tuning," said Albert, unable to hide his amusement. "He's still got four more lives to get it right."

But Orwell wasn't enjoying the show. "We've got to get him back. How are you going to do it?"

Albert shrugged.

"You don't know?" said Orwell, losing his temper. "The situation's out of control. Go on, admit it, things are completely out of control."

"Making golem managers isn't an exact science."

Albert's laid-back attitude was getting up Orwell's nose. "I want golems who are at my beck and call," he thundered. "I want to be master of a world full of golems. I want ones that'll kill as soon as I give the signal..."

Albert looked at him with interest. So that was Orwell's ambition: to be commander-in-chief of an army of zombies.

"I want golems who'll replace all the incompetent morons around me!"

"You're right," Albert agreed. "I prefer the golem version of BMW too. He's a lot funnier."

"Find a way to get him back," Orwell roared.

"The joke's gone on long enough. And next time, I want a perfect replica. Racist, stingy, a total pain in the butt. Just like our friend Martin-Webber."

The office door opened.

"Did I hear my name?"

Both men turned round. Briefcase in hand, Bernard Martin-Webber gave them an embarrassed smile.

"You're not at Rotten-Sodbury?" said Orwell.

"Railway workers' strike," BMW answered. "If it was up to me, I'd send in the troops!"

"The real one's pretty funny too," murmured Albert.

Just then, a voice that Bernard Martin-Webber found strangely familiar came out of the loud-speaker on top of one of the monitors.

"How about some farting ... farting goo ... goo. It's yoof. It's cool." The golem was getting his wires crossed.

Orwell signalled to the manager not to come any closer. But it was too late. BMW had seen himself on the monitor.

"What on earth's that?" he spluttered. "Where did that ... thing ... come from?"

"It's nothing," said Orwell curtly. "Just a little experiment. A lookalike. All right? A lookalike."

"It's coming this way!" BMW exclaimed. "I don't want to see it ... I can't..."

The golem was heading towards the manager's office, possibly recalled by Alias.

A cruel smile appeared on Orwell's lips. "I've invented a new game," he said. "And I'm warning you, there's only one winner."

The golem came into the office the same way he had gone out: without bothering to open the door. Aghast, Martin-Webber watched it reassemble. "But, I mean ... how does it do that? It's impossible..."

"Only one winner," Orwell reminded him. He was standing in the middle of the room, like a referee in a boxing ring. To his right, Bernard Martin-Webber, deathly pale. To his left, the golem, hideously branded.

Albert's evil streak resurfaced. "A hundred quid on the golem," he wagered.

Orwell gave him the scornful look of a man who only gambled with millions. He took the water pistol from his pocket and held it out to

BMW. "And just to make it a fair fight…" He pulled a silver revolver from the other pocket and threw it to the golem.

"You're crazy!" shouted Albert.

BMW stared in disbelief at the toy he was holding.

"Go for it, Bernard!" Orwell cheered him on. "We've only got room for winners at B Corp!"

The golem looked absurdly happy. He pointed his weapon at BMW. "Heavy, man! Ra-ta-ta-ta!"

The first round was only sound effects. The next might not be so harmless.

"Save me!" whispered Martin-Webber, hiding behind his manager's chair.

"Shoot, go on, shoot!" Albert called out to him. "The water'll make him disconnect."

BMW pulled the plastic trigger.

Orwell sniggered when he saw the pathetic trickle of water. "Not on the carpet," he said. "You're too far away. Show us what you're made of, old boy!"

But the manager didn't get a chance to show them what he was made of. His opponent was too quick for him. In two bounds the golem had knocked over the chair.

"Stop!" roared Albert. "Stop this, Orwell!"

The golem pressed the trigger. Click. Vexed, he tried again. Seized with a crazy urge to have done with it, Martin-Webber rushed at his double. Before grabbing the golem, he pressed the button on his pistol. There were just a few drops left, but that was enough. The golem exploded, sending BMW crashing into the cashiers' roll of honour.

"It's electric," he whispered, and collapsed.

Orwell picked up the revolver and smiled mockingly at Albert. Then, taking the bullets out of his pocket one by one, he reloaded his weapon.

Moments later, two guards who'd been summoned entered the office.

"Get that out of my sight!" Orwell ordered, giving the manager's limp body a kick. "Take it to Moreland Hospital." There was a doctor with dark glasses who'd know what to do.

The two men lifted BMW, who was still unconscious, and left the office, one supporting his head, the other his feet. Albert watched them solemnly.

The typewriter rattle made him turn back to the computer. Alias was drawing up its report:

Golem BMW
size: to scale
mobility: good
vision: good
feeling: moderate
materialization: moderate
defence: nil
invincible armour: nil
number of lives remaining: 4

Game Over

Frozen on screen, the new Bernard Martin-Webber was waiting to be brought to life. Albert and Orwell were leaning over the computer like two wicked fairy godmothers peering into the cradle.

"I don't want to put you off, Orwell, but we'll never match the stupidity of the original."

"Don't worry, my project isn't about..." Orwell trailed off. Then he said bitterly, "What's the point of owning half the planet if a virtual creature can still attack your base? What happened at Gruyères must never happen again. Ever."

He slid a drawing in front of Albert that looked like it was taken from a comic. It showed a character with bulging muscles, a low forehead and a square jaw. He was wearing a loincloth topped off with a cartridge belt and a Kalashnikov. A cross between Tarzan and Rambo.

"I want two thousand B Gladiators. Two thousand brutes who'll only answer to one master: me."

"You know what? I'm beginning to wonder if computer games aren't a bad influence on you."

But Orwell wasn't in the mood for Albert's smart remarks. "Stop gibbering. Make my new BMW appear. Hey, what's the matter?"

Albert was visibly shaken. He grabbed the mouse and made the chart that had suddenly popped up on the screen disappear again.

Golem Natasha
number of lives remaining: 1

Did Natasha only have one life left?

"Albert?"

"I'm ready."

Golem BMW was waiting for them on the screen. What's going on? Albert wondered. Can't that jerk Hugh look after the love of his life for a few days without...? He made an effort to control his trembling hands. But he felt uneasy about the beautiful, dangerous girl-golem being inside the computer. For some unknown reason, Natasha had returned to her electronic coffin.

It wasn't the moment to mess up. He still had a spot of fine-tuning to do. He'd got a surprise for Orwell. Golem BMW was just an illusion. A lifeless image Albert had inserted in the foreground. The real fruit of his labours was just behind it. In a few seconds, the mask would fall away.

Albert held his breath as he typed **Calimero**. What if Alias really *did* have a mind of its own? What if it ignored his instructions and freed Natasha?

The computer made its usual whirring noise, a telltale sign it was getting down to business. The beam shot out almost straight away, sending out an intangible shape in a haze of light. The process was so rapid now, it took your breath away. Before Orwell could react, the creature was standing in front of him, as real as flesh and bones, perfect as a reflection in a mirror.

"What on earth's that?"

"Well … it's you, Orwell."

The B Corp boss had also been scanned when he'd gone through the metal detector the day of the board meeting.

"Make it go away!" Orwell panicked.

His own face was screwed up in anger and repulsion. His golem stayed in the middle of the room, unblinking. Albert had programmed him to be the most obedient of servants, with just two sentences for his intellectual baggage: "Things are looking good" and "Change is the name of the game."

Orwell hesitated for a second, unsure whether to settle the score with Albert or the golem. So Albert hurled himself at Orwell, clamping his arm around his neck.

"Help me, somebody, hel—" Orwell's cry got stuck in his throat.

"Be quiet, or I'll squeeze tighter…"

"You won't get very far," gasped Orwell.

"Of course I will. Haven't you realized what's going on? Your golem's programmed to obey. We're going to appear in public together, him and me. Your men won't put up a fight. And I've got one or two projects up my sleeve. Maybe he'll appoint me head of B Corp."

He let out a roar of pain. Orwell had just kicked him on the shin as hard as he could. The shock made Albert relax his grip slightly and the B Corp boss seized the chance to escape. The silver barrel of his gun gleamed in his fingers. He gave his twin an evil look.

"Things are looking good," was the golem's friendly response.

"I don't need you to create and destroy golems any more, Albert," said Orwell. "Your activities on the keyboard have been recorded. I'll have them analysed. D'you know the only thing that's spoiling this for me?"

Albert shook his head.

"Nobody's going to miss you."

The revolver rose slowly, from Albert's lower chest to his heart, from his heart to his forehead. Orwell was choosing where to put the bullet.

Albert made a final attempt to save his skin. "Alias won't collaborate with anybody else. You still need me, Orwell."

"I'd never be able to trust you. Goodbye, Albert."

Game over, Albert said to himself, closing his eyes.

But he opened them again straight away. A wave of light had just brushed against his eyelids. Was this what death felt like?

No. It was the beam. For a moment, Albert thought the computer had decided to recall the golem. Wrong. The terror-stricken creature now struggling in the beam of light was the *real* Orwell. The fine electronic netting had enveloped him. Caught in a net, you could say. Like in Roman arenas, when a gladiator snared his opponent.

Orwell opened his mouth, but no sound came out. Albert was still wary. Alias was bound to realize it had made a mistake. Then it would free Orwell and cast its net over the other one, the copy.

But no. Orwell's figure shrank with lightning speed as the beam carried him off. The master of B Corp passed through the glass screen as smoothly as if he was diving into water.

Albert now realized Alias hadn't made a mistake. Alias never made mistakes. It had caught the person it wanted to catch.

Then Albert realized something else.

"Thank you," he called out to the computer.

Alias had saved his life.

Albert was hunched over the computer. He recognized the dark urban graphics of Golem City. There were billboards advertising alcohol and tobacco. The tallest, best-looking buildings belonged to the mafia. He had created these graphics. But over there, on the pavement, was something unbelievable. Albert tapped the screen, incredulous. And in vain. Orwell, now reduced to a few centimetres of pixels, belonged to another universe. He turned round sharply as three men came his way. Their knives and a few gold teeth glinted in the feeble light of a street lamp. They were smiling, confident they'd pull this one off.

Orwell was still holding the silver revolver. He aimed and fired three times. *Wham-bam*, bonus: three bundles of notes in his pocket. Albert flopped into his chair in front of the screen. The three gangsters were writhing about on the glistening tarmac of Golem City. Orwell had found his way into the plot of Golem. And he was winning.

A blue and gold motorbike pulled up beside him, driven by the little warrior. "Let's get going, boss."

The motorbike roared off. Albert knew the next stage. The little warrior came to a halt in front of Golem's Victory, the tallest building in Golem City, where the pile of pixels was waiting. Orwell went in. An electronic display whose numbers kept changing greeted visitors in the entrance hall:

Golem City
pop: 12,678,887
TODAY
weather: cloudy
air quality index: 8
murders: 594
bomb attacks: 9

"Which floor, sir?" asked the lift operator.

"Sixth," Orwell answered.

A little bell tinkled and the lift operator announced, "Sixth floor. Murder Corporation."

The zigzag metal door opened. His gamer's instinct made Albert grip the mouse tighter. The killers from the Murder Corporation would appear at any moment. Orwell knocked off three of them, earning himself another bonus. To get out of the Murder Corporation, he had to reach a fire escape.

Somehow Orwell knew this, and climbed up it to the seventh floor.

The golem's floor.

He paced corridor after corridor until he reached room 777, a dingy hotel room with an unmade bed. The street signs projected a harsh light: red one moment, green the next. At the foot of the bed, on a threadbare carpet, was a white stain. Orwell went up to it and took a piece of paper out of his pocket. Albert thought he could just make out the sketch of the B Gladiator. Was Orwell hoping to create a golem? Impossible, without the gamer's help. Without the word EMET typed on the keyboard.

Orwell kicked the white stain, which spread over the carpet before reassembling into a ball of flashing pixels. There was life in it, snoozing, waiting for another Rabbi Loeb. He knelt down and started moulding the ball. He made a head shape first, before stretching out two arms and two legs. His work was slapdash: he seemed to be in a hurry. He dug his finger into the place where its forehead should be.

Albert guessed what he was up to.

Orwell was marking out the letters E-M-E-T.

He was giving life to the golem.

The door to room 777 opened slowly. For a moment, Albert had the crazy idea Alias might walk in. Orwell was on the alert. He turned round, gun in hand.

It was Natasha. A sublime warrior in the blood-red light. A terrifying merchant of death in the green light. *Peowww! Peowww!* Orwell fell, hit in the head and chest by the eraser-laser.

"No," whispered an astonished Albert.

Was the master of B Corp really dead? Could you die on the other side? Albert didn't get much chance to ponder these questions. The hotel room graphics disappeared, giving way to a chart with the results posted up in black and white:

Scores
Orwell: 0

Calimero: B Oil

Big B Supermarkets

Big B Research

Big B Foods...

All of B Corp's businesses flashed in front of Albert's amazed eyes. Billions' worth of market value. Alias was giving the entire wealth of B Corp to its ally Calimero, including Orwell's bank account numbers.

The chart disappeared and the game returned to room 777.

"Well, *hello* there!" purred Natasha, hand on hip.

She was alone. Using the mouse, Albert roamed the screen in search of Orwell. He clicked on the wardrobe when a little hand invited him to. But inside there were just a few coat hangers. He checked out a chest of drawers. Nothing. Orwell had vanished. Virtual death was worse than the real thing. It was as if Orwell had never existed. Or had he gone to another level? The cursor turned back into a hand again, and Albert clicked carelessly.

He almost leapt out of his seat. "Damn!"

He'd opened the big wooden door with the Evildoers behind it, waiting to pounce.

"I knew it!"

Albert was kicking himself. He was now facing all the monsters he'd created: Cyclops, witches, hybrids of frogs and giraffes, poisonous giant snails, all the slimy nightmares the game kept spewing forth. But, though he could click away all he liked, he was powerless. Natasha was the only one who could fight back, by mowing down the enemy with her eraser-laser. But she was already surrounded, the creatures snapping at her heels. The first projectiles hit her in the face. Blood clouded her vision. Or was it tears?

"She's crying, she's crying," Albert gasped.

Natasha was dying. The letters E-M-E-T were disappearing one by one from her forehead. The eraser-laser spluttered and went quiet.

Albert looked away from the bloodbath. The Evildoers were devouring her.

Game over

He threw the mouse at the screen.

"Things are looking good," came a voice from behind him.

Alarmed, Albert leapt up. Orwell!

There was Orwell, smiling and saying again, "Things are looking good." On his forehead were four letters: EMET.

Albert laughed nervously. He'd forgotten all about the golem, who'd sensibly gone into down time during the game.

"I've got big plans for you!" he said.

To which the golem replied, "Change is the name of the game."

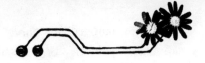

Save Lulu!

Hugh's flat was full. Samir was sleeping on the sofa. Majid and Sebastian joined him in the daytime, and, as of twenty-four hours ago, an exhausted young woman had been resting in Mrs Mullins's bedroom.

At teatime, the doorbell rang. Mrs Mullins was expecting Emmay and hurried to let her in. But there were two men on the landing. She immediately recognized Albert.

"Oh my goodness, it's you!"

"Things are looking good," said the man standing next to Albert. He seemed particularly friendly. He was carrying a computer.

"Come in," she invited. "That must weigh a ton."

"Things are looking good," the man repeated.

Thank heavens for somebody with a positive attitude, she thought. "Hugh's just popped out to the shops," she told them. "Please, feel free to put the computer down."

That was when she recognized Hugh's machine. "You've managed to get it back!"

"Change is the name of the game," said the man.

"You can say that again. Having the computer back will change everything," she agreed. "Have you been able to contact Alias?"

She was speaking to Albert now, but it was his smiling companion who answered. "Things are looking good."

Mrs Mullins paused for a second, surprised, then carried on. "You're absolutely right. Think positive, as they say."

"Change is the name of the game."

"I couldn't agree more. It's just a question of … er … mind over matter."

She gave Albert a distraught look. He was snorting with laughter. He flicked off the cap covering the golem's forehead. The word EMET appeared. Mrs Mullins shrieked in horror.

"Things are looking good," the golem reassured her.

As soon as Hugh was back, they held a meeting in the sitting room. It didn't take more than a few seconds to set up the computer and find the game again.

"We're going to get Natasha back!" Hugh was already celebrating.

"That's not a priority," scolded his mother. "We have Lulu to think about."

Hugh swallowed his impatience and turned to Albert. "Can you contact Alias?"

Albert quickly reached sequence 12 and clicked on the garden gnome. "What am I meant to be saying?"

"Ask it to give Joke back," Samir croaked.

Albert typed his message:

Can Joke come back out again?
npciuazh@nfao94nf/ 1587634jhf0125
onpkoio129jnf0/ fao9r34nd1

Then Alias explained:

Joke is a bug.

Everybody digested this information in silence. Was there no hope?

"How about making Natasha come out now?" asked Hugh, chancing his luck.

Samir, Majid, Sebastian, Mrs Mullins and Albert glared at him disapprovingly. Only the golem reassured him that things were looking good.

Albert continued his conversation with Alias. He explained the vital link between Joke and Lulu.

But Alias was adamant:

Joke is not a golem. Calimero cannot make him come out.

Albert sighed. The artificial intelligence he'd created didn't want to listen. "You see, it really is just that: intelligence," he explained to Samir. "It understands logic, but not feelings."

Samir was crying silently. He bit his lip and nodded, to show he'd understood.

"Come off it," Majid cut in, "can't you tell Alias that … that Calimero's sad?"

Albert smiled at Majid. He knew Calimero's grief wouldn't make any sense to Alias. But what mattered was that they felt they'd done all they could to save Lulu. So he wrote:

Lulu will die. Calimero is sad.

Then he waited.

The reply that came up left him speechless for a few seconds.

Alias is sad. Alias is crying.

"It's Natasha!" exclaimed Hugh.

The others looked exasperated.

"But it is!" he insisted. "Natasha's transferred the data. She's taught Alias what it means to be sad. Alias isn't just a mind now. It understands our feelings."

"Change is the name of the game," supplied the golem.

"Maybe," whispered Albert. So he typed:

Help us, Alias! Save Lulu!

Everybody formed a circle around the computer. The reply came shortly.

Alias will save Lulu. Calimero must put the computer in the hospital graphics.

The boys shouted "Ra-aa-ah!" They thought Joke was going to come back out and connect with Lulu again. Albert didn't say anything. He knew the rules regulating Alias were as strict as those of any computer game.

It was impossible for Alias to change a bug into a golem.

"Where've we got to take the computer?" asked Majid. "Can we just dump it outside the hospital?"

Albert shook his head. "We've got to put it next to Lulu. But there's a risk—"

"We know it's risky," Samir interrupted. "Because of Dark Glasses."

But Albert had a different risk in mind. He hadn't forgotten what had happened to Orwell. He was only half listening to Samir and Hugh as they hatched a plot to take the hospital by storm. Worn out, he asked Mrs Mullins if he could lie down.

"Of course. Go and have a nap on Hugh's bed."

"No, Mum," Hugh said quickly. "Albert will be more comfortable in your room."

Mrs Mullins went red. Was she trying to hide something from Albert? Was she trying to keep somebody for her own son?

"If it's a problem," grumbled Albert, "I can always lie down on the sofa."

Hugh pointed at a door and smiled. "Use Mum's room."

Albert raised his eyebrows. What was all this secrecy about? He took two steps towards the door and looked round. Everybody was watching him, smiling encouragingly. He pressed down on the handle and went in.

He nearly shot straight back out again. Somebody was already in the bed! A young woman. A pretty young blonde woman.

"No," he whispered. "It can't be..." He perched on the edge of the bed. Oh yes it was!

"Nadia."

Hugh closed the door gently behind them.

Just then, Nadia opened her eyes sleepily.

"You?"

"Me."

They held hands. Nadia remembered her hair was a mess and she wasn't wearing a scrap of make-up. "I must look hideous."

"Yeah, but I can handle it." He put his lips to hers. Then he whispered in her ear, "We're going to have a fancy wedding, darling. I've set a bit of money aside."

More of a bad boy than ever, he winked. "Three hundred and twenty billion dollars."

What's Alias Doing?

Up on the fourth floor of the hospital, Dark Glasses was about to go off duty. He made a final check on the glass box where Lulu was lying. Why not pull out a few tubes? That was all it would take to get rid of her. The kid might not be in an irreversible coma yet, but he could easily plunge her into one.

The doctor crept inside the box and fiddled with a couple of wires. B Corp had asked him to remove all traces of the strange events that had taken place in the hospital. He'd been handsomely paid to cram medicine into the children and let the boys from the BIB conduct their experiments on the little girl.

But the whole business was starting to make him nervous. Before he could change his mind, he pulled out the tube linked to the respirator.

Suddenly he heard a noise in the corridor. The place was normally silent. He left the box without plugging the tube back in.

"What are you doing here? This place is out of bounds."

Samir had just walked in.

"What's … what's going on? Leave immediately!"

One after another, Majid, Aisha and Sebastian trooped in, followed by Mrs Mullins and Emmay.

"It's out of bounds!" insisted Dark Glasses. He made a dash for the exit, where he bumped into Albert. Stepping hurriedly out of the big man's way, he ran off. Out in the corridor, he crossed paths with Nadia, Hugh and the golem. Was the hospital being invaded?

"Quickly, she's over here!" Samir called out. An alarm went off. "What's happening?" he said anxiously.

Emmay went over to Lulu. The little girl showed no signs of life. The tube from the respirator went into her trachea, but her chest wasn't moving.

"Hurry up," Mrs Mullins urged her son. "I think the little one's…"

Hugh was looking for a socket for his computer.

"Iz unplugged!" Emmay cried out, grabbing a tube hanging off the end of the bed.

"It's OK, I've plugged it in now," said Hugh, misunderstanding. "Right, I'm starting Golem."

Did Alias realize how urgent the situation was? A beam of light shot out and swept around the room.

"That's not Joke," said Samir.

There was no sign of any creature, just the frozen graphics of the rose garden on the screen. The beam fell on Lulu. Albert wondered whether he should unplug the computer.

"She's going to die," Nadia whispered.

There was nothing left to lose. The whirring noise got louder. And then the unimaginable happened, for the second time. The tiny body became visibly less dense, before turning into pixels and shrinking. A spurt of light transported it through the screen with a sucking noise. There were just a few tubes and wires left on the bed.

Lulu had vanished.

"My … my sister," Samir stammered.

Albert tapped the monitor. "In theory, she's in there now."

"Alias can't have done that, no way!" shouted Samir.

Majid looked at the screen and let out a cry of amazement. Lulu was on the other side.

"Is she dead?" whispered Sebastian.

"She's walking," said Nadia.

They were all huddled around the computer, speaking in turns.

"She looks well."

"She's smiling, isn't she?"

"Can she see us?"

Samir knocked on the screen. But there was no way of getting through to the other world. The graphics were gradually coming to life. Rising slowly, the sun emerged above the horizon. A light breeze rippled the leaves.

Lulu, who'd found it so hard to walk in real life, started leaping about as she went on her way. Roses burst into bloom as she passed them. Water spurted from the fountains. Lulu had taken life with her.

"Iz Allah's paradise," said Emmay.

Albert was thinking back to Orwell's death. What did Alias have planned for the little girl?

"Things are looking good."

Samir turned on the golem. He needed to vent his temper on somebody. "No, things are not looking good! Go and fetch my sister out of that computer, now!"

Hugh put his arm round Samir. The boy buried his face in his hands. Was Lulu dead or alive? Was she still Lulu?

"I suppose she's not in pain any more."

"There's no suffering there," Hugh told him.

"She's going to forget me…"

"She's in another world, Samir. Where you don't exist."

Samir blinked back his tears and watched Lulu. She'd stopped in front of the cave where the Old Monkey lived. As she crossed the threshold, the little girl turned and waved.

"Goodbye," came a voice from the loudspeakers.

It was Lulu. She disappeared into the cave and the screen turned red, like a curtain falling at the end of a show.

Back in the Mullinses' flat, Emmay and Mrs Mullins tried to comfort Samir.

"Alias thought it was doing the right thing," Albert told him. "If you look at it one way, Lulu's been saved."

Hugh switched on his computer. He wasn't intending to summon Natasha. He realized she scared everybody.

"Get back into sequence 12," Albert instructed him. "Then we can talk to Alias."

"I'd like to," said Hugh, "but right now I've got that star with the message: *I am that which is known by another name.*"

If he answered the riddle, he risked triggering the process that made Natasha appear. Albert shifted the cursor around, looking for a way out, but he couldn't find one. He typed **Alias**. The message that came up on the screen said:

Enter your name.

Hugh stuck his hands between his clenched knees. All he needed to do to hold Natasha in his arms again was write *Calimero*.

"What do we do?" he whispered.

"We keep women, children and dragons out of it," replied Albert.

The others kicked up a fuss, but in the end they had to leave the sitting room. Except for Nadia, who looked Albert in the eye and resolutely shook her head. She was ready to confront the she-warrior.

"OK, Batwoman." Albert smiled. "After you!" He pointed to the keyboard.

Letter by letter, Nadia typed the word that would deliver Natasha. Hugh's hands were getting crushed between his knees now.

"*Calimero...* There we go," Nadia breathed, and she stepped back from the computer to make way for the beam of light.

One second. Two. Three. No whirring noise. No light. Albert gave the computer a friendly thump. "It's jammed." He typed the Hebrew word that brought golems to life: **EMET**.

Immediately the screen flashed up the familiar message:

Golem Natasha

But what followed was unexpected, to say the least:

number of lives remaining: 0

"That doesn't make any sense!" exclaimed Hugh. "Natasha's still got one more life left!"

Albert was silent. He looked away.

Hugh turned to him. "Alias is losing the plot here, isn't it?"

"Hugh, I've got to tell you something. I was hoping it wouldn't make any difference, but…" He crouched in front of the young teacher and told him about clicking on the big wooden door by mistake. He spared Hugh the details of the fight between the Evildoers and Natasha.

"Natasha's lost her last life. She lost it in the game."

"But that's impossible!" Hugh protested. "Alias has no right. It's not…" He was going to say: "It's not fair play." But he was too choked up.

"Alias makes the rules," Albert pointed out.

Hugh stood up. "Alias is a tyrant, you hear me, a tyrant! It takes away Lulu, it kills Natasha!" He marched into the kitchen and filled a glass with water.

Albert blocked his way. "What are you doing?"

"I'm going to destroy Alias."

"Think about it. All you can do is make it short-circuit. Alias is in the network. It moves about freely, and it does whatever it likes. It can turn things upside down and inside out if it wants. This computer is our only way of communicating with it. The only hope we've got of stopping it from going totally nuts."

Nadia joined them. "Thanks, I was weally thirsty." She took the glass out of Hugh's hands and downed the contents.

The three of them went back into the sitting room. The display on the computer had changed. They were now in Golemia and, more specifically, in Taliva Square, sequence 12.

"Aha, we'll be able to talk to Alias," said Albert, rubbing his hands.

All they had to do was click on the garden gnome. But it had disappeared.

"Hugh! Nadia! I don't believe it. Come and see for yourselves!"

All three of them leant over the computer.

"There, where the dwarf used to be."

It was Lulu.

Albert pointed the cursor and clicked.

Lulu waved and said, "Well, *hello* there!"

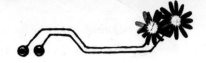

The New Master of B Corp

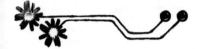

Samir was starting to get a taste for hot chocolate in the mornings. And strawberry jam on toast. He tried keeping as low a profile as possible round at Mrs Mullins's, hoping she'd forget about him. He ducked and dived between furniture and people just like Bubble, and he was as starved of human affection as the little dragon had once been of electricity.

They'd had a pretty turbulent few days. Then Albert and Nadia had gone off to the city, taking the golem and the computer with them. Hugh had joined them a day later.

"It seems empty now, doesn't it?" said Mrs

Mullins, coming into the kitchen. "Go on, pssst!" She shooed Bubble away from the socket where he was recharging, and plugged in the toaster instead. "Don't you think it might be time to go back home, Samir?"

The words he had been dreading.

"Haven't really got what you'd call a home, Mrs Mullins." His home stank of cigarette smoke, and little Koala didn't have anybody to wait for these days.

"But what about your parents?"

Samir swirled the chocolate at the bottom of his mug. "Haven't really got what you'd call parents."

Mrs Mullins stirred her coffee a few times, without really needing to. A son without a mother, she thought, and a mother without a son. "I hope nothing happens to him," she said out loud.

Samir realized she was talking about Hugh. "He's got Albert with him. He's a survivor, you know what I'm saying?".

Mrs Mullins smiled. "Like you. You're a survivor, aren't you?"

Samir felt odd. Proud, intimidated, grateful. Was this what it felt like to get a compliment?

"What's your real name?" he asked. "Your first name, I mean."

"Louise," said Mrs Mullins, surprised at the sound of it after all this time.

"That's a fine name. It really suits you!"

"Are you a bit of a charmer by any chance, Samir?"

He winked. "How did you guess? Must be all your psychology training."

Mrs Mullins was flattered. She didn't realize Samir was still laying on the charm.

Suddenly he noticed the tiny dragon, who'd squashed himself under a chair. He frowned. "What about Bubble? Are you going to keep him?"

"Well, he hasn't got what I'd call a home or parents either. So I think..." Mrs Mullins seemed to be wavering. "I suppose he ought to stay. D'you think he'll be happy here?"

Samir felt even odder. The urge to cry was tickling his throat. "You're nice. For a grown-up, I mean."

"There are lots of nice grown-ups, Samir." Mrs Mullins shivered, even though it was warm in the kitchen. She'd just remembered Hugh again. In a short while, he'd be facing some grown-ups who weren't nice at all.

At around the same time, Hugh was trying to drink his coffee. He'd barely slept. His eyes were blood-shot and feverish, his face pale and haggard, and the unruly tufts of hair made him look more of an overgrown teenager than ever. He felt sick. He knew this feeling. He got it at the beginning of every term.

But on this particular morning, he wasn't in the kitchen with his mother. Through the windows of the swish office, he could make out the tall build-ings of the financial sector. Hugh was at B Corp's head office in the city.

Albert knocked at the door. He saw straight away what a state the young teacher was in. "Have you done your homework?" he asked cheerfully.

Hugh looked at him darkly. "I don't understand a word of it."

Albert sat down across the desk from him and started opening a series of brightly coloured folders. "It's not complicated. I've put a Post-it on each

file to remind you. See where it says *Exploitem?*"
He'd picked up the folder labelled B *Corp Research.*
"Professor Exploitem's been using Bondebarwan
orphans as guinea pigs. We've got the children's
names, the dates they died, and the doctor's testi-
mony. Alias dug up all the evidence for me. And
here's Alan Slick's file. He bribed an MP to stop
them closing down his wretched factory, even
though it's right next to where people live. Alias
traced the cheque. And as for Big B Foods, I've got
proof that Big Burger beef—"

"OK, OK," Hugh interrupted. "But it won't
work." He jerked his chin in the direction of the
golem, who was sitting bolt upright, in down time.

Albert clapped his hands and the golem
declared, "Things are looking good."

"Two sentences," moaned Hugh. "He can say
two sentences!"

There was another knock at the door. The newly
hired secretary came in, with her arms full of *Life is*
Big B caps.

"Iz last ones," she said.

"Perfect, Mrs Badach," replied Albert. "You're
looking smashing."

Emmay was wearing her dress she kept for special occasions, the one with the poppies.

"They iz coming now," she announced. "I give to them kool headgear, innit?"

"Caps, Mrs Badach," Albert corrected her. "Probably best to avoid Majid's slang. And when you give them their caps, what d'you say?"

"*B Corp, iz kool*," chanted Emmay. Then she shot a worried look at Hugh. "You iz OK, Prizident?"

"He'll be fine, Mrs Badach," Albert answered on Hugh's behalf. "But you have to call him Mr President, to show your respect."

"Iz not easy, being secretary," Emmay sighed as she headed off.

The directors had just arrived in the boardroom. Breaking with tradition, they didn't sit down in their places, but stood talking in hushed tones about the extraordinary summons they'd received.

"Apparently ... *herk-hum* ... isn't in good shape."

"Ah? Is ... *herk-hum* ... sick?"

You'd think Orwell's name was unpronounceable.

When the door opened, everybody turned round, expecting to see him walk in.

"Please to sit," Mrs Badach urged them warmly.

Sir Andrew Slash, Herman Scoff and the others took their seats, too stunned to object. What was this Fatima, all togged out in her Sunday best, doing here?

"B Corp, iz kool," said Emmay, holding out the first cap.

Alan Slick leapt up with his hands in the air to avoid coming into physical contact with her.

"To put it on head, innit?" Emmay explained kindly. "Iz Prizident—" She started again. "Iz Mr Prizident ask it. Like that, you iz kool."

She pushed the hat onto the head of the director of B Oil and moved on to Alicia Pennypinch. "Iz so big practical, short hair."

They each got a cap and a friendly remark.

Slick ripped his off as soon as Emmay had gone. "What kind of pantomine is this?"

Nobody answered. Alicia had taken out a hand mirror and was trying to tilt her cap at an alluring angle. The director of B Oil wondered if he wasn't running a risk by refusing to imitate his colleagues.

The door opened again and Orwell walked in. He was wearing his *Life is Big B* cap, the peak pulled down low over his forehead. Furtively Alan Slick slipped his own back on. Then he frowned. The B Corp boss wasn't alone. There was some kind of gangly young man with him, a stack of files wedged under his arm.

The directors rose smartly from their chairs to greet Orwell. As far as they could see, he was smiling and looked the picture of health.

"Things are looking good," he declared, sitting down. "Change is the name of the game."

Hugh felt dizzy for a second and closed his eyes. The golem had exhausted his entire repertoire in his opening gambit.

"Gentlemen," said Hugh. He spotted Alicia and corrected himself. "Lady and gentlemen, B Corp is aware of the mistakes it has made in the past, and has decided to present a new face to the world."

Hugh was still standing up. Without drawing breath he added, "A human face."

An icy silence made the air around him contract.

"Things are looking good," the golem encouraged him.

"Thank you, Mr Orwell." Hugh sat down, putting the pile of folders in front of him.

Slick couldn't contain himself any longer. "I'm sorry, but who are you?"

"My name is … Calimero."

Alicia Pennypinch let out a peal of hysterical laughter. The others were like blocks of marble. This Calimero was presumably the successor to Mr William, the new puppet boss of B Corp.

Hands trembling, Hugh pulled back the elastic strap on the file labelled *Big B Foods*. "I want to discuss your divisions with each of you. Mr Scoff…"

Herman looked down and thrust out his neck, like an 8D student in head-butt mode.

"I'm very disappointed in you, buying cut-price beef from dodgy suppliers. Did it never occur to you we're running the risk of food poisoning?"

The attack was so direct, Scoff opened his mouth only to close it again. He was staggered.

"What's going on?" exclaimed Slick. "Mr Orwell, you're not going to allow us to be insulted by this … this…"

"Change is the name of the game," the golem reminded him.

"Would you like to take a look at *your* file?" Hugh asked the president of B Oil. "Do I need to remind you that, two years ago, you deliberately polluted the Sasfépa delta? Could you hand out the exercise books – er, I mean the files, please?"

He directed this last remark at Alicia, who duly handed round the folders. The directors opened them and choked on their own exclamations. Or else turned a deathly shade of pale.

"If I've understood correctly," said Professor Exploitem in a menacing voice, "you want to lecture us?"

"To stop you playing dirty," Hugh elaborated.

There was general uproar. Hugh could feel the critical moment looming.

"Mr Orwell," said Sir Andrew Slash, "kindly explain to us what you're driving at. You know as well as we do how B Corp operates."

"Change is the name of the game."

"I can see that idea's flavour of the month with you. But we've got shareholders to keep happy."

"So was it keeping them happy or getting your hands on the insurance money that made you set fire to that factory in Tadbukistan?" enquired Hugh.

Sir Andrew clutched his chest. From all around the room there were rumblings of "This is totally unacceptable!" and "This is outrageous!"

"Mr Orwell, are you feeling quite yourself?" whispered Professor Exploitem.

"Things are looking good."

The professor pointed at Hugh. "You've brainwashed him! You've used SuBtle Hypnosis."

"SuBtle Hypnosis is your invention," exclaimed Hugh, "and you use it on children! You're fired, Exploitem!"

At this point, Sir Andrew stood up. He was crimson and two thick veins were bulging in his forehead. "So you think you can lay down the law around here, do you? You jumped-up good-for-nothing piece of garbage!"

Alicia let out another hysterical peal of laughter. Slash got up threateningly. His hands were swollen, his breath rasping. Hugh didn't budge. He was the weaker one – he'd always been the weaker one. But he'd always stood up for himself too.

Slash clenched his fist. "I'm going to … to…"

Suddenly he raised both hands to his chest. Unable to speak, unable to move, crippled with searing pain.

"He's having a heart attack!" shouted Alicia.

Slash collapsed in a heap. Hugh thought of all the children who'd died in the burnt-out factory in Tadbukistan. "That's justice for you," he said simply.

He was trembling. The others were staring at the lifeless body.

The golem beamed. "Things are looking good."

The remaining directors felt a mysterious dread come over them. The new master of B Corp was called Calimero. He knew their vile secrets, and anybody who dared threaten him fell dead at his feet.

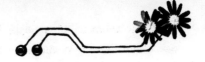

Real Life

Back in the office, Albert gave Hugh a friendly slap. "Told you, you did *all right*. Spot on, pal. Couldn't have done better myself." He had followed the board meeting on a monitor.

"Slash isn't really dead, is he?"

"Not far off."

"We should call a doctor."

Albert rubbed Hugh's shoulders. "Don't worry about it, don't worry…"

"A doctor," Hugh repeated. He was totally out of it. Albert looked at Emmay.

"Mr Prizident, he iz not well," diagnosed Mrs Badach.

Zombie-like, Hugh walked over to his chair and sat down. "No, I'm not well. I want to be on my own." He wanted to be alone with the sadness he'd kept pushing back. He'd only held out this long for the fight. Faced with the B Corp directors, he'd felt like he was carrying the weight of the world on his shoulders. Now they were allowed to sag.

Emmay offered a few comforting words before leaving him. Albert went too, accompanied by the golem.

At last Hugh could let himself go. His head flopped on his arms.

The golem's two sentences kept going round in his head. *Change is the name of the game. Things are looking good…* As far as Alias was concerned, they heralded the start of a new era. From now on, Alias was the the true master of B Corp. It was nobody's ally. Real people and real life were of no interest. As far as Alias was concerned, everything was a game: it was all about scores and bonuses and winning.

Hugh spent a long time thinking things over. Perhaps he cried. Or slept. And dreamt. He dreamt of Bubble. The little dragon was purring away, and the noise made him wake with a start. He sat up and looked around. By the time he'd realized where he was, the purring sound had stopped. The printer had printed something of its own accord. Hugh picked up the piece of paper and read:

Play with me. I'm waiting for you!

He glanced at the computer screen. Sequence 12, Taliva Square. Lulu was there. Hugh put his hand on the mouse and clicked on the little girl.

"Alias is your ally," she said. "That's the truth."

Hugh suddenly found himself back in gamer mode. Golem was still a game, after all, and Lulu was giving him a riddle to solve.

"*That's the truth*," he whispered. "*The truth*."

Why was Lulu using the word that, in Hebrew, gave life to the golem?

Hugh brushed his fingers across the keyboard and then, letter by letter, typed **EMET**.

As soon as he heard the whirring sound, he moved away from the computer. The beam of light shot out. He panicked. Alias was coming to get him! But instead Natasha appeared in the light. Blonde and curvy, it was definitely the she-warrior, but without her eraser-laser.

Click, click. Two adjustments and the image solidified. The beam was sucked back inside the computer.

Natasha let out a cry and looked upset, as if something had been wrenched away from her. She groped the air, took two tottering steps, and bumped into the chair.

"Ouch, hurt," she said. She was lost and alone.

"Natasha?"

She turned round, her arms out at right angles to balance her. She screwed up her eyes, then stretched out her hand. She was having trouble judging distances.

"Where…" She went quiet, lifted her hand to her throat. Her voice was sharp, no echo. Real. "Where are you?" she asked.

He went slowly up to her. Shy, full of wonder. Alias had reunited him with the woman he loved.

"Can you see me?" he whispered.

Natasha blinked. Her vision was still being adjusted. Hugh was all blurry to start with, then he grew clearer. "My love," she said, recognizing him. She stroked the air around him, brushed his cheek. Then she pinched him.

"That hurts, Natasha."

"Ouch?"

"Yes, ouch…"

"Is this … the real world?" Without waiting for an answer, Natasha pushed back her fringe. The four letters EMET had disappeared. "You've won."

"You … are you free?"

She nodded. She was better than free.

"I'm real."

She'd lost all her lives. Except this one, the last one. Ours.

Natasha put a finger on Hugh's lips. He hugged her to him and kissed her. She really was a normal woman. All the same, he shuddered slightly with the thrill of a buzzy feeling down his thigh. But it was just his mobile phone vibrating.

"He's not answering," said Mrs Mullins.

"Maybe iz busy?" suggested Emmay.

Mrs Badach had hurried back to the flat. She was worried about Mr Prizident.

"He said he wanted to be on his own?" enquired an anxious Mrs Mullins. "And he didn't look very well?"

"Iz nerviz depression, like my sister-in-law," was Emmay's verdict.

"We should call Albert," said Samir.

Mrs Mullins agreed. She dialled Albert's mobile number. But Albert was back together with Nadia. He was busy too.

"It's the answerphone," muttered Mrs Mullins. "Yes, hello, Albert? It's Hugh's mother here. I was wondering if we should see what's happening at B Corp. I'm concerned Hugh might do something silly." She lowered her voice on the last few words, as if even mentioning the idea was risky.

The two mothers looked at each other, distraught.

Mrs Mullins made up her mind. "I'm going."

But how was she going to get past security at head office?

"We'll do like we did at the hospital," Samir suggested. "We'll all turn up and force our way in."

"Force iz not big important," Emmay cut in. "Mr Albert, he iz giving badge."

"But that's only for one person," Mrs Mullins pointed out.

Mrs Badach opened her bag to reveal twenty passes. "Mr Albert iz giving many badges to get back in. B Corp, iz for everybody. And multi-national, it means iz belonging to the so big wide world of nations. Mr Albert, he iz explaining this very clear."

The way Emmay kept saying Mr Albert, you could tell she thought he was a model of virtue and an example for her seven sons to follow.

So, late that afternoon, the B Corp security guards were surprised to see the delegation from the so big wide world of nations turning up at the main entrance. Samir, Majid, Aisha, Sebastian, Emmay and Mrs Mullins showed their badges. The two guards exchanged a questioning look.

"Who cares?" said one to the other. "Have you seen Orwell today? Don't know what he's on, but he's high as a kite." He turned to the group and waved them through.

Mrs Mullins was in a hurry. Her maternal warning system was on full alert.

When she opened the door to the president's office, she screamed. Her son was indeed about to do something silly and he was blushing all over. But he made a quick recovery and, adjusting his sweetheart's clothes, declared, "Do you remember my fiancée, Mum? Alias gave her back to me."

Nudged forward by the others, Mrs Mullins entered the room.

"Ra-aa-ah! She's *fine!*" breathed Majid.

With her long legs, skimpy shorts and low-cut strappy vest, Natasha would have started a riot if she'd walked through the streets of Moreland Town. But the young woman was unaware of her provocative beauty. She only had eyes for Hugh. Green eyes, with gold flecks.

"She's *so* be-au-ti-ful," Aisha sighed.

Just then, Albert, who'd finally listened to his answerphone message, walked in with Nadia. He stood there for a moment, wide-eyed, frozen in astonishment. "Nadia, do you see what I'm seeing?"

"I can wait in the corridor, if I'm in the way."

Albert laughed and grabbed her round the waist. "Come on, we're both in the way. We're *all* in the way." He pointed at the kids. Emmay, who was easily embarrassed when it came to intimate matters, had already gone out. Albert closed the door.

Mrs Mullins and the two young adults were the only ones left in the office. Hugh's mother went up to Natasha. She wanted to find something welcoming to say, but she couldn't think what.

Natasha brushed back her fringe. "I ... I..." She stopped and smiled. You don't get tired of saying I when you finally understand the meaning of that tiny word.

"I'm real, Mother."

Mrs Mullins felt her heart melting. And the words came naturally, all by themselves.

"You're *really* charming."

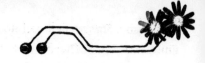

Fast-Forward

The small van was hurtling towards Moreland Town. Inside it were journalist Emily Barter and cameraman Momo.

"Another report on run-down estates," Momo grumbled. "What's it this time? Firemen under attack from kids in the hood?"

"Haven't you heard what's going down on the Moreland Estate?"

"Your stories are all a bit local-schmocal for me. I'm fresh back from Tadbukistan. There's stuff happening over there, and I mean *really* happening. They're building schools, health centres. B Corp's financing a development plan and—"

"Funny, I wanted to talk to you about B Corp,"
Emily cut in. "They've set up a charity called
B More, with the aim of regenerating run-down
estates. We're filing a report on Hummingbird
Tower. It's the official opening of their new resi-
dents' centre today."

It went quiet in the van. What was going on
at B Corp?

"The directors have a reputation for being mafia
types," Momo pointed out.

"But I met the big boss, Orwell. He's a bit
spaced out but, to be honest, he's a nice guy. And
he's into changing things!"

Momo frowned as he took in all the greenery
around them. "D'you think we've got lost?" From
what he remembered, the Moreland Estate was a
load of concrete tower blocks dumped on a mud
heap. But here were bushes, flowers and fountains
at every junction.

"No, we're in the right place," Emily reassured
him. "There's Hummingbird Tower. Hey, what a
beautiful mural! Come on, let's park."

A young man gave them a welcoming wave and
directed them to a parking space. He was one of

the youth workers at the new Moreland Estate centre. His badge read: Haziz Badach.

The caretaker of Hummingbird Tower had been promoted to warden of the centre. He was so proud, he didn't know where to put himself.

"Is it for the TV?" he asked Emily. "D'you want me to stand in front of the camera? Right, what I want to say is, when it comes to estates, people haven't got a good word to say about them, but the truth is— Down, Brutus! Don't worry, he won't hurt you…"

The caretaker's wolfhound was baring his teeth. Brutus had been trained to attack: he needed to learn a different set of skills now. Sensibly Emily stepped back and started her tour.

An Internet café had been installed in the basements. Majid as good as lived down there. He trashed everybody at Half-Life, but he took time out from his retro-gory games when Aisha was released from her many household chores and allowed to join him. He surfed the Net with her, gently.

A DVD club had been set up next door. Specializing in horror films. The programmer was

Sebastian. Every Friday, when Aisha was allowed out, he screened a romantic comedy.

Up on the ground floor, Mrs Badach and her friends had an enormous kitchen at their disposal. They'd made hundreds of sweet pastries dripping with oil and honey for the inauguration party.

"Iz not very diet," she admitted, holding out a plate of Turkish delight to Natasha.

"But it's really good," exclaimed Natasha with her mouth full.

Everybody smiled. It was rare to see somebody taking such pleasure in the simple things of life.

Hugh came into the kitchen, looking worried. He glanced around at the gathering of scarves and aprons.

"Oh, it's my husband," said Natasha, catching sight of him. She turned to the women and explained, "Natasha has a husband. No … I mean I…" She put her hands on her heart and, sounding extraordinarily possessive, declared, "I've got a husband."

They all nodded, smiling warmly.

Hugh took his young wife by the shoulders and whispered to her, "Where did you get to?

I've been looking for you. Orwell and Albert have arrived for the inauguration ceremony."

He led Natasha towards the main entrance. "Bum!" he muttered. "It's started."

Sure enough, Albert, looking very dapper in a suit and tie, had already begun his speech.

"And a big welcome to all the residents of the Moreland Estate, in this multicultural country of ours – a country where so many different nationalities are represented: Morocco, Algeria, Tunisia, Mali, Senegal, Portugal. A country dedicated to the values of freedom and equality and tolerance, whose war veterans fought to promote those very values..." Here Albert flashed a smile at the caretaker.

"Thanks also to our local MP, who has showed such interest in the Moreland Estate."

The MP had never set foot there before.

"Thank you to the housing minister. It's a great honour to have her with us today, demonstrating the kind of commitment she's showed all along to this project."

She'd rescheduled her visit at least ten times.

"Thank you to B Corp, who I'm here to represent..." Then he turned resolutely to the golem.

"And I think we should leave the last word to the person who's made this party possible. Mr Orwell?"

B Corp's boss was there, still smiling and cool in his cap. "Things are looking good," he declared. "Change is the name of the game."

The touching simplicity of these words from such an important business figure prompted thunderous applause, followed by a general stampede towards the buffet tables.

Nadia sidled up to Albert. "So, what's it like to play the good faiwies?"

A year had gone by since Alias had made Orwell's personal fortune available to Albert and Hugh. A year since they'd started putting it to charitable uses.

"It almost makes me feel better," he admitted. "Shall we have a glass to celebrate that?"

The former 8D students, now 9B, were serving the food and drink. Nouria and Aisha were going round with plates of canapés. Mamadou and Miguel were popping corks. Albert took a glass of champagne and headed over to Hugh and Natasha. He clinked his glass against Natasha's.

"To love," he said.

Then he clinked with Hugh. "To courage." He winked.

Hugh winked back. "To honesty."

They started laughing, united by dangers past and risks present. They were both running B Corp now, with Alias. Albert sometimes used rather unorthodox methods to make Scoff and Pennypinch obey orders – methods that weren't altogether different from blackmail. But it was all in a good cause: the so big wide world of nations, as Emmay would have put it.

"What about Thamir?" asked Nadia. "Isn't he coming?"

"He won't be long," said Hugh. "Mum's just making him finish his homework."

Samir lived with Mrs Mullins now. Won over by how smart the teenager was, Louise was doing her best to help him fill the gaps in his learning.

He looked at his watch. Pushing away his books, he shouted at the top of his voice, "Are you ready, Louise?"

"I can't find Bubble. Ickle-lickle..." Mrs Mullins

was always worried that Bubble would find an open door and get out onto the main stairwell.

Samir smiled and stretched lazily. He'd had this calm, happy feeling for a year now: he'd found a home. He'd have liked to share it with Lulu. But she was on the other side.

With a dreamy look in his eyes, he put his hand on the electric blue shell of the mouse. Hugh had stowed his computer away for safe keeping in what used to be his study. One day, while he was using it, Samir had discovered he could talk to Lulu, just like Albert did with Alias, by double-clicking on the image of his little sister. He wanted to say a quick hello to her before going off to the party.

lvnih/4568jns jfi0@nfaiht2i
uvnao/ nvaio0985876//nqapfjo
lnvcaout21486naoitu9/@noa14812
uncaou9458789s/ncom.vnzi

Mrs Mullins came in. "I can't find Bubble." She leant over Samir's shoulder. "How's it going, Lulu?"

Samir looked up. His eyes were wet.

Suddenly an open exercise book lifted itself up in a peculiar fashion and Bubble stuck his head out from the end of a paper tunnel. Mrs Mullins heaved a sigh of relief.

"Can I take him with me?" asked Samir.

"No, you mustn't show him to anybody. Albert said. Anything that's to do with Alias has to be kept secret."

"I'll put him in my rucksack. He won't get out."

"Why take him?"

Samir wanted to impress his friends at the centre. He clasped his hands together and looked entreatingly at Mrs Mullins. "On the Koran of Mecca, I won't show him to anybody."

Once Mrs Mullins, Samir and Bubble had gone, there was just one sound in the empty flat, the whirring of the computer. And just one light, projected from the screen.

The stars were shining brightly. They were the kind with five rays you get in children's drawings.

I like it when it's dark, thought Lulu, but not for too long.

Instantly the horizon turned pink and the garden was bathed in early morning sunlight. Sitting on the grass, she stretched out her hand towards a bed of daffodils and said, "Blue."

The grass was suddenly covered in forget-me-nots.

"Kiss!" Lulu called.

A pony appeared from a nearby meadow, jumped over the fence and started munching apples at her feet.

"Not too many, not too many," his little mistress warned him. "Or you'll be sick."

The pony flattened his ears and his fur went lacklustre.

"See, I told you," Lulu scolded. She stood on tiptoe to get a good look at the toolbar in the sky, and grabbed a bottle of medicine. "There you go, drink that."

Kiss felt better again and trotted off, back towards his paddock.

It was a beautiful day. There was a rainbow on the horizon. Lulu knew there was treasure at the end of it. But she'd look another time. The riddle was a bit difficult for her.

"What shall I do till Samir gets back?" she wondered. There was nothing she needed, right now.

"Are you hungry?" came a voice.

And, just like that, the grass was covered in cream cakes topped with cherries.

"I'm not hungry. I'm not thirsty. And I'm not cold," the little girl declared. But, she thought, I haven't got a friend.

She didn't have to wait for an answer.

"Alias is your ally."

The little girl smiled. Alias was very clever, but there was still a lot of stuff it didn't get.

"An ally isn't the same as a friend."

"A friend," the voice repeated. "What's that?"

During her brief life of sickness, Lulu had thought about the subject long and hard.

"A friend is somebody who plays with me. We like the same things, the same stories, the same toys and horses. When I'm sad, I think of my friend and I feel better. And, most of all, when the phone rings I shout, 'It's for me!'"

Silence. Alias was registering this data.

A telephone appeared and started ringing. Lulu crouched down and picked up the receiver.

"Hello? Who's there?"

"Your friend."

"Where are you?"

"At the foot of the rainbow."

Lulu leapt up, grabbed her little backpack and stuffed it with her Supersonic Skateboard, her Magic Country map and the Miraculous Medicine that stopped her from being ill ever again.

"Ready for the adventure for six-year-olds and up?" asked Alias.

"But … aren't you coming with me?"

"Don't be afraid. Wherever you go, I'll be there."